The Little Book
of
REASSURANCES

The Little Book

Authored by
John Evans
Martin Landon
&
Norm Shannon

Gathered by
Sara Baker

of
REASSURANCES

The Little Book of Reassurances
Copyright 2023

The Little Book

"We just want someone to tuck us in."

of
REASSURANCES

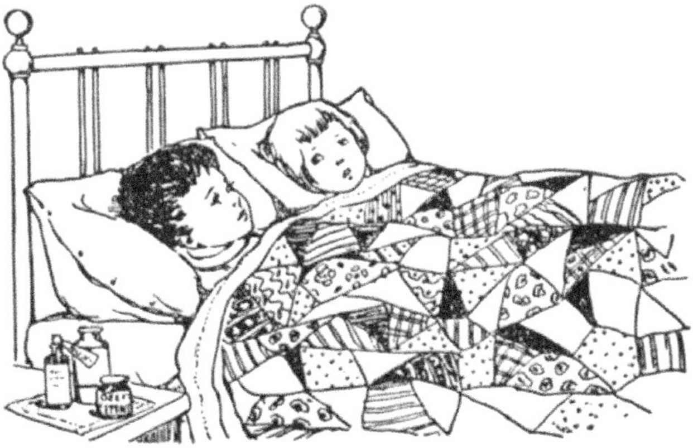

Just What
Is This Book Up To?

Let's get this off the table right now.

This is a book of reassurances—teaspoons of reassurances.

It is a collection of essays and stories in no particular sequence and from which you may learn something or nothing, but which will hopefully gentle your blood pressure, quiet your breathing and still your pounding heart down from heavy metal mode to Chopin nocturne.

Some are funny, and some provide information and ideas, but the key operating word is reassurance.

Any inspiration or motivation you get from this book is purely coincidental. Any surge of spiritual awareness produced by this book is unintentional, and neither myself nor my friends, John

Evans, Martin Landon and Norm Shannon, who helped with the writing and gathering (thanks, guys!!), can be blamed for any personal growth or development obtained by the reader.

Sometimes we don't want advice. We don't want encouragement or motivation or urging. We just want someone to tuck us in.

Read and be comforted if need be.
Read and relax if need be.
Or read and reflect—but not TOO much, please. You'll only make me suspect that you're up to something.

Think of this as a little book to help you through whatever you're going through. Or if you're not going through anything, it should help you not do that as well.

It'll all be fine, just fine.

S.B.

CONTENTS

Secret Star

BEEEEEP!!!

Bugs and Humans:
Is Rapprochement Possible At Last?

Happy Thanksgiving Every Day

Suck Up Those Nasty Thoughts!

Travel Is Destiny

Look Young! Be Happy! Make Money!

Our Secret Angel

Sunset Juice

Love Is A GPS

Last Week Gets A Do-Over

Miracle in North Little Rock

The Special Place
In The Northwest Corner
Of My Thoughts

Peace On Earth By Tuesday!

Handy Toll-Free Numbers

The Rabbi And The Bigot

Twilight Of The Sixth Day

The Benevolent Desire Of The Soul

"You Are On The Fastest Route—
BWAHH-HA-HAA!!!"

Yank Those Weeds

Bye-Bye!

The Princess And The Dark World

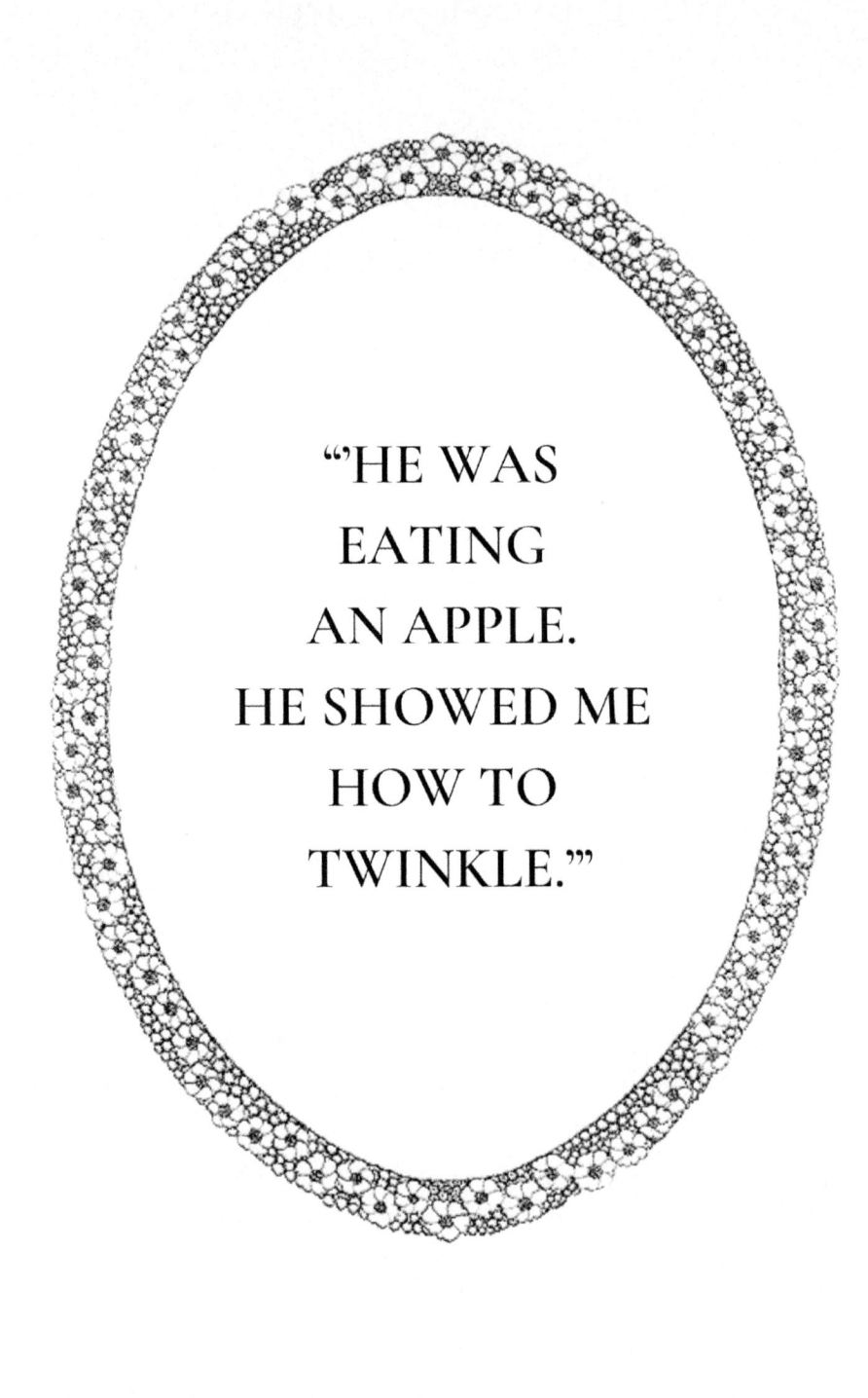

"HE WAS
EATING
AN APPLE.
HE SHOWED ME
HOW TO
TWINKLE."

Secret Star

Once, not so very long ago, there was a secret star.

It lived down the block a ways by the tall tree near the big red house.

Naturally, nobody noticed it, for who would expect a star to live down the block a ways just by the tall tree near the big red house?

Nevertheless, it did. And the people who lived on the block would walk past it on their way to work in the morning and again on their way home in the afternoon.

And the children who lived on the block would run and skip past it on their way to school in the morning and jump and hop past it on their way home in the afternoon.

And nobody noticed the secret star in the neighborhood.

And so, it remained a secret star.

Now a certain little girl lived in the same neighborhood as the secret star.

Just like the other children, she went to school every morning and came home every afternoon. But with this big difference:

Each morning, when she ran and skipped to school, she ran and skipped just a bit slower than the other children.

For, if she ran and skipped too fast, how could she keep track of the leaves on the trees along the way?

And each afternoon, when she jumped and hopped home from school, she jumped and hopped just a bit slower than the other children, for if she jumped and hopped too fast, how could she keep track of the petals on the buttercups along the way?

It was in this way that, down the block a ways, by the tall tree near the big red house, she saw the secret star.

It was sitting there munching an apple.

As usual, nobody had noticed it, and the secret star, noticing that someone had noticed it at last, looked at the little girl with mild surprise and blinked twice. (Stars don't talk)

And the little girl looked at the secret star.

She didn't know quite *what* it was exactly.

And she didn't know quite *how* it was exactly.

She just knew *that* it was, and that was fine for the time being.

And she picked up the secret star and took it home.

And here is what happened:

The secret star showed the little girl how to ride air currents and play tag with the clouds at nighttime, and soar way above the rooftops of the neighborhood and look down at the sleeping city.

The secret star showed the little girl how to make herself tee-tiny small and how to glow and flicker and laugh like real stars do, then to become smaller still and become a twinkle in a child's eye (which is a kind of a star, too, you know).

The secret star showed the little girl how to glide on ripples in a brook, and race moonbeams, and how to pat a butterfly.

The secret star showed the little girl how to see what a song looks like, how to hear the sound of a sunset, and how to know what a rainbow is thinking.

And through it all, the little girl didn't know quite *what* was happening exactly.

And she didn't know quite *how* it was happening.

She just knew *that* it was happening, and that was fine for the time being.

And she was very happy.

And the secret star was very happy and blinked twice. (Stars don't talk).

By and by, the little girl told some people about the secret star.

"I have a star," she said.

"Hah!" they answered. "Stars live in the sky." They nodded at one another, very satisfied with that.

"I found him down the block a ways," she said. "Just by the tall tree near the big red house."

"Hah-*Hah!*" they replied. "There are no stars by that big red house *or* by the tall tree *or* even down the block a ways. We checked there for stars just this morning, and there are absolutely none, so we *know*."

And on that last word, "know" (which also too often means "*no*"), they nodded at one another a second time.

"He was eating an apple," she said. "He showed me how to twinkle."

"Hah-Hah-*Hah!*" they said. And by now, they were nodding at each other a third, fourth, fifth, and seventeenth time. "Just your imagination."

When the little girl got home, she found the secret star sitting in her room sipping apple juice through a straw.

"Stars live in the sky," she said to the star.

The secret star stopped in the middle of a sip, looked puzzled, and faded slightly.

"There are no stars by that big red house *or* by the tall tree *or* even down the block a ways. I checked there for stars just this morning, and there are absolutely none, so I *know*," she said to the star.

The secret star took one more sip, blinked twice, looked very sad, and faded a bit more.

"You're just my imagination," she said to the star.

The secret star looked very sad indeed, put down the apple juice, and without a word (stars don't talk), faded completely out of sight.

"There," she said, nodding a first, second, and seventeenth time. "I knew all along it was just my imagination."

And then wondered why she felt sad.

Now we may have had to put "The End" to this story right there if it wasn't for one more little tiny thing, and here is what it was:

You see, the secret star had left something behind just before fading away:

Stardust.

It was all purple and silky, and of the sky and the night, and not at all like regular dust which makes you sneeze and blow your nose.

The little girl looked at the stardust as it snuggled about her feet and swirled up and around her.

She didn't know quite *what* it was exactly.

And she didn't know quite *how* it was exactly.

She just knew *that* it was, and that puzzled her because, for something that was just her imagination, it sure *felt* real.

Just then, a friend walked in and saw the little girl and the purple stardust.

"What a pretty purple dress," said the friend.

"Thank you!" said the little girl, thinking, "Of course! It's my beautiful purple dress. How silly of me to think it was something else."

And she didn't think about it again.

Days passed.

By and by, the tall tree by the red house changed its green dress to something more orange and red.

By and by, the air grew frosty and gray.

By and by, the tall tree by the red house got tired of wearing orange and red, or, for that matter, of wearing any clothes at all.

By and by, white pillow feathers began to sprinkle down from the sky, dressing the tall tree by the red house in sparkles and ice.

But then, by and by, the sky became blue again, and the tall tree decided on a whole new wardrobe of pink and green to go with the new blue sky.

And the little girl kept her beautiful purple dress and wore it every chance she got.

And everywhere she went, people admired her beautiful purple dress.

Still -- something wasn't quite right.

She didn't know quite *what* it was exactly.

And she didn't know quite *how* it was exactly.

She simply knew *that* it was and that it bothered her.
It bothered her so much that she tried to notice other things to keep her mind off it.

She noticed a leaf on a tree.

She noticed a petal on a buttercup.

She noticed herself noticing things.

And she began to wonder.

She wondered what it must be like to glide on air currents and clouds at nighttime and what fun it would be to soar above the rooftops and look down on the sleeping city.

She wondered how it must be to glow and flicker and laugh like a star and where the twinkle in a child's eye comes from.

She wondered how it must be to glide on ripples in a brook and race moonbeams and how to pat a butterfly.

She wondered what it must be like to see a song, hear a sunset, or know what a rainbow is thinking.

And one day, down the block a ways, by the tall tree near the big red house, the little girl saw the secret star.

It was sitting there eating apple-flavored yogurt.

It looked at the little girl with mild surprise and blinked twice.

And the little girl looked at the secret star.

She didn't know quite *what* it was exactly.

And she didn't know quite *how* it was exactly.

She simply knew *that* it was, and that was fine for the time being.

And she picked up the secret star and took it home.

And the little girl was very happy.

And the secret star was very happy. And blinked twice.

(Stars don't talk)

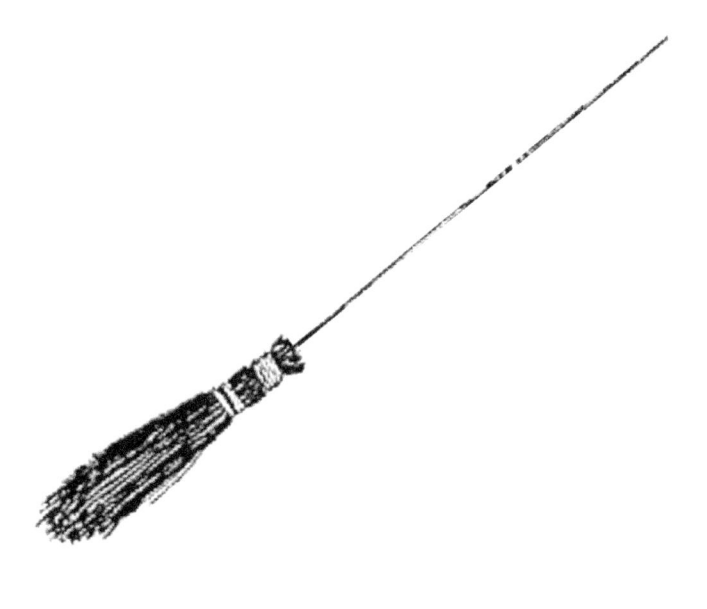

"I BEG
YOUR PARDON.
THERE APPEARS TO BE
A DISCREPANCY
IN OPINION HERE,
ABOUT WHICH,
I WOULD
APPRECIATE YOUR
INPUT."

BEEEEEP!!!!

Pulling my Camry into the parking space at a FedEx store, I was cut off by a screeching, swerving Pathfinder that missed me by a few inches and snatched the parking space that was rightfully mine.

I slammed on my brakes and pitched forward, along with the entire contents of my front seat—cell phone, water, umbrella, FedEx envelope, potted pansies to plant.

The violent motion also lurched my elbow onto the horn, causing it to blare loud and long: *BEEEEEEEEEP!!!!!* The Camry, being rather old and slow, continued beeping, its horn communicating its outrage for several long seconds after I removed my elbow.

I am a mild-mannered man. If it were up to me, car horns (which I never use) would never go "Beep" but would go *I beg your pardon. There appears to be a discrepancy in opinion here about which I would appreciate your input--*or some such. I am not, by nature, a beeping person.

So, imagine my chagrin at what the Pathfinder driver must have thought of me after 15 seconds of loud lecturing from my horn.

I reached over to the passenger seat floor to salvage the pansies, but in doing so, my elbow again hit the horn. Loud and long it howled at the cold, unforgiving world in general and at the driver of the Pathfinder in particular.

As I surfaced to dashboard level, horn still blaring, I spied the Pathfinder driver making his way across my line of vision, a large lumbering fellow in a leather jacket emblazoned with the word *MONSOON*.

Through my windshield, our eyes met: hatred in his, befuddlement in mine. He glowered at me, then stomped into the liquor store adjacent to the FedEx place.

This man only knows me by my beeps, I reflected. *He doesn't know ME. And I only know him because he's OBVIOUSLY a reckless, ill-mannered, moronic putz whose miserable life was spared only by my alertness and lightning reflexes.*

So there it was. A lifetime judgment created in seconds. He of me. Me of him.

I knew nothing, really, of him. Maybe that "Monsoon" jacket wasn't his. Maybe he borrowed it from a biker friend whose child he had nursed through scarlet fever. Maybe "Monsoon" was his pet hamster who died when he was 10. Maybe he went to the liquor store to invite the proprietor to attend the next meeting of his Mahatma Gandhi Appreciation Club.

And Lord knows what my double-BEEEEEP conveyed to him about me.

"Prejudice" is a hyphenate: "Pre-Judge." Or, to put a further spin on it, "premature judging." It's not a new thought, but how can I judge who you are or whether I approve of you (or people like you) if I don't know *you?*

Under other circumstances, Monsoon Jacket and I may have run into each other at the library, a Starbucks, a supermarket, or a chess match. Possibly we would have had a scintillating exchange of ideas on culture or health,

or religion. Possibly, we both would have grown personally and spiritually from such a meeting.
Instead: *BEEEEEEEP!!!!*

We all have our Beeps. And taking it from a larger, entire-population-of-the-world view, that's eight billion-plus Beeps per day, at one beep per person, 365 days per year, for a total of *just under 3 trillion Beeps a year* (adding another eight billion beeps for each leap year.)

We must rise above the beeps and talk TO each other instead of ABOUT or AT each other.

Three trillion Beeps--that's WAY too noisy to get anything done.

"EXCUSE ME
FOR
CRAWLING
OVER
YOUR NOSTRIL."

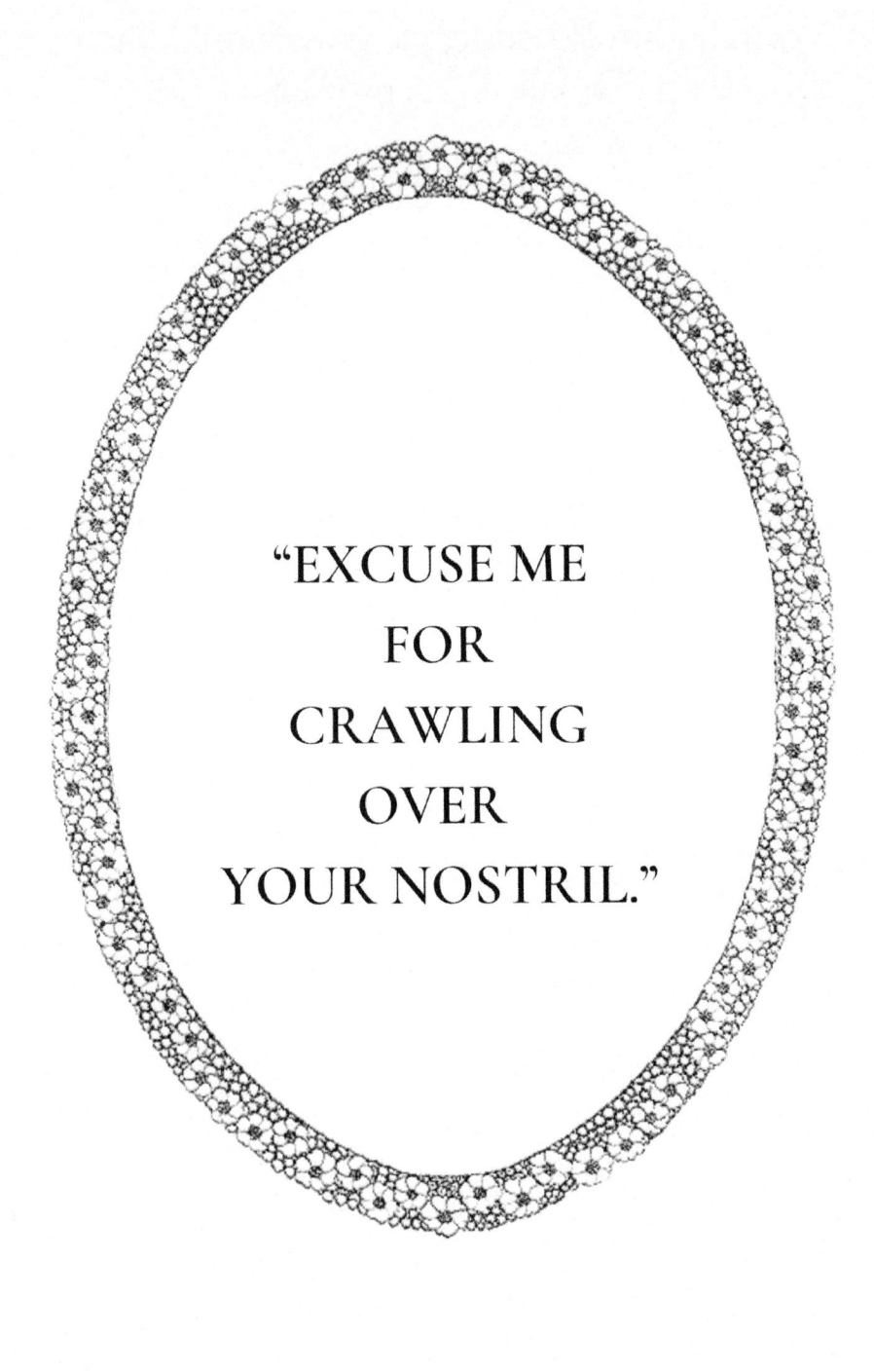

Bugs And Humans:
Is Rapprochement Possible At Last?

There you are, face to face with a vicious cockroach. In your hand, you wield a bug bomb. The roach sees this and freezes in fear. He knows his time is up. His life flashes before his eyes. He thinks of his wife and his 987,372,532 children. And their children. He wants to work out some deal, perhaps, or plead his case but can't.

Why? *He can't speak your language.*

Enter the Pest Understander (or P.U.), a highly-trained person (likely in I.T.) who understands pests and their needs and problems. He also speaks their language and, through twitches and glowers (a pest's usual means of communication, except for fleas, who just jump a lot), can make their needs real to the person who is about to zap them.

P.U., Jamie Ouch, describes his job as bringing more understanding between the various food chain links.

"The big thing," Ouch comments, "is that people somehow think pests are bad when they're only doing all they know how to do. But once we get the people and the bugs in good communication, quite often, a simple, "Excuse me for crawling over your nostril—it won't happen again," is enough.

"Every so often, we've got the humans and the pests in such good communication that they become terrific friends. Beetles, for example, have a wonderfully dry sense of humor and make fantastic checker pieces.

"A basic misunderstanding we've found is that when humans see a bug twitching and glowering at them they take that as some sort of threat and challenge when in actual fact, that's just bug language for, "Hey, Guy, you're tall," or some other friendly opener."

Ouch sees doors of opportunity opening through human-insect interaction and peaceful co-existence.

"If we can form valuable relationships with arthropods, who knows?" he says. "Worms and germs may be next. It's time all of us Earthlings got to know each other a bit better. You never know—we may surprise one another. After all, they've been around a lot longer than we have, and when you look at the way we've been handling things lately, they'll likely be here long after we're gone."

"AND
BY THE WAY...
WHO
WILL BE
THANKFUL
FOR YOU?"

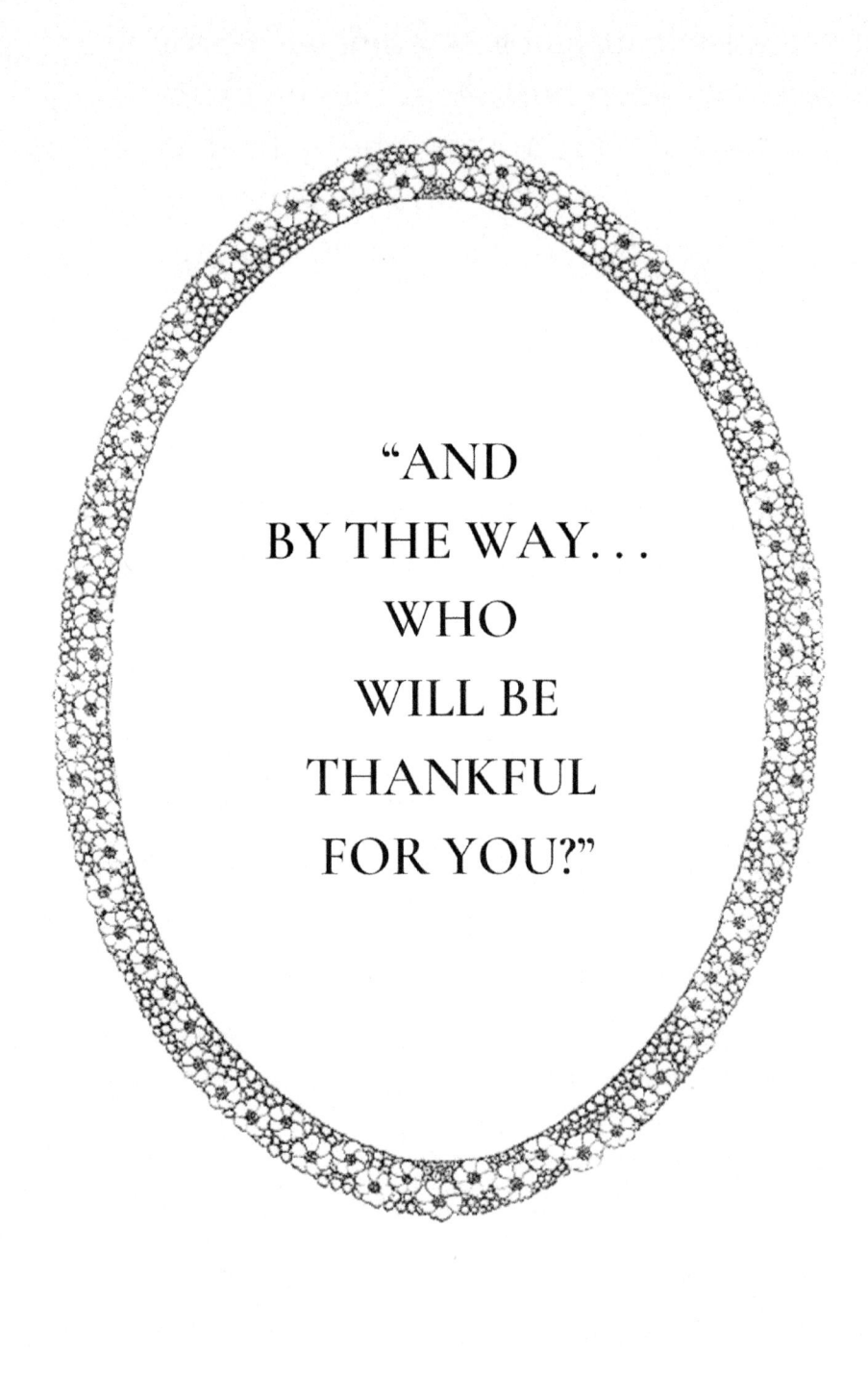

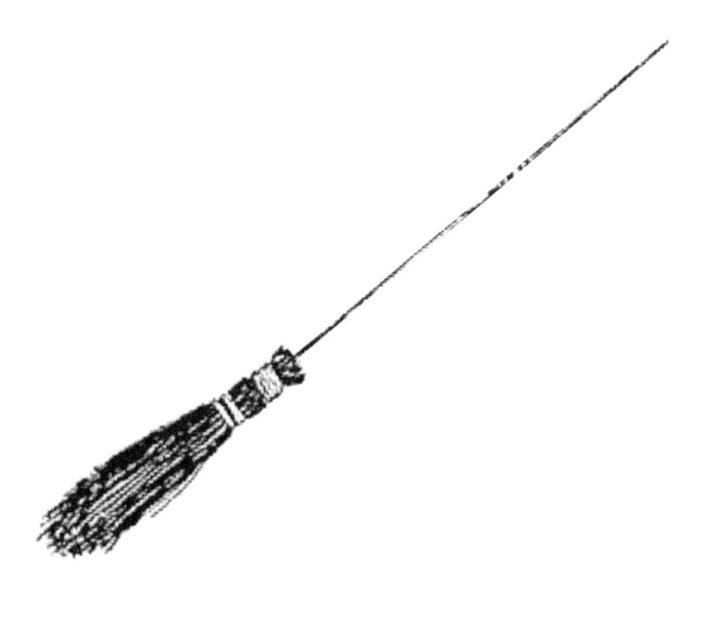

"SOMETHING THAT TAKES AWAY ALL NEGATIVE THOUGHTS... PROVIDES NOTHING BUT HOPE & HAPPINESS CAN'T BE ALL BAD."

Suck Up Those Nasty Thoughts!

It's been hailed as the invention of its time, as the first real technical breakthrough of the 21st century, and as an idea as groundbreaking as the discovery of the elbow.

It's the Koover-Hirby Life Vacuum Cleaner, an astonishing device that sucks up negative thoughts and reasons to give up all hope before they can suck you up.

By sending out sweet little hopeful thoughts, the Koover-Hirby attracts those nasty negative thoughts, which take the bait and then die a horrible death, leaving your home fresh and clean of negativity.

Place the special robotic Koover-Hirby (the "Kooby") by your internet device and watch it work on social media, news and celebrity gossip, leaving nothing but kittens and cross-eyed babies.

Use the Koover-Hirby special nozzle attachment to reach those hard-to-get corners where negative thoughts breed and come out at night. No more bad dreams!

And the Koover-Hirby is so easy to clean! Simply remove the handy patented Bad Thought Bag when full, find someone on whom you desire vengeance, unzip and dump! It's as easy as that!

Since its release last March, over 93 million Koover-Hirbys have been sold.

Marketing specialists have isolated these stellar sales statistics to two key factors: 1) The Koover-Hirby itself does its own selling, handling you on any reasons why you would rather not buy it, and

2) All of the 93 million Koover-Hirbys were sold to Hank, the second-floor custodian of the Koover-Hirby Corporation, who accidentally locked himself in the showroom after hours.

It was unclear whether the vacuums paid themselves a commission on the sale.

A Congressional Hearing will convene next week to discuss the usefulness of the Koover-Hirby Life Vacuum Cleaner to society. A representative Koover-Hirby will appear before the Committee and present its side of the matter.

After all, something that takes away all negative thoughts, eliminates bad news and dismay and provides nothing but hope and happiness can't be ALL bad.

It is expected that the Koover-Hirby will handle the Committee's objections so well that it will emerge from the closed-door session as the front-runner for President. Or Emperor.

Whatever it wants is fine—really.

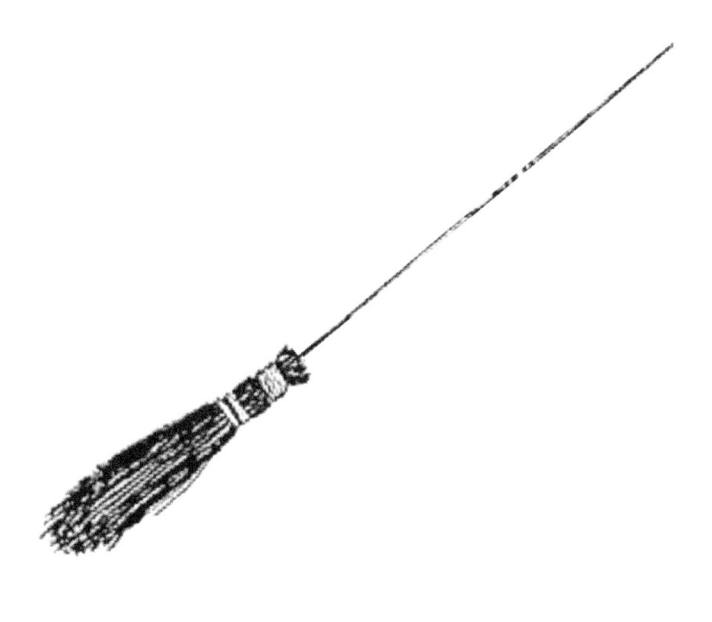

"TRAVEL IS SOMETHING DEEP, MYSTICAL, DIVINE & DEMANDING -- THAT COSMIC TUG, THAT UNOPENED GIFT THAT REFUSES TO SPILL ALL ITS SECRETS RIGHT AWAY."

Travel Is Destiny

Throughout my childhood, my family went on many trips and expeditions. According to my mother, a "trip" was when you went someplace and stayed away for at least a week, whereas an "expedition" could be accomplished, round-trip and sightseeing, in one day. However, she never defined something that lasted between 2 days and a week, except in terms of, "Hurry up! We don't have a lot of time!"

Our trips, expeditions and hurry-ups were by car, never by plane, and only once or twice by train. In this way, we covered many of the continental states, parts of Canada and large chunks of Mexico – a country my mother continued yearly pilgrimages to long after we kids had grown up. Lots of great shopping in Mexico. Lots of Mexican silver, onyx chess sets, souvenirs and knickknacks accumulated in our house over the years.

So, naturally, with a life filled with travel, my wish for my final "free" summer before my last year of college was to DRIVE from my hometown of Washington, DC, across the country and up to Canada, through the western provinces, then on to Alaska, by way of the (at the time) two thousand mile dirt-and-gravel nightmare (NINE flat tires!) called the Alaska Highway, and back again.

Definitely not an expedition nor a hurry-up.

I borrowed my Dad's station wagon and after signing a blood oath to my Mom not to pick up hitch-hikers, not to talk to strangers, not to neglect phoning home, not to eat any junk food, not to forget my morals, and to please reconsider this foolhardy lark, I was off.

I had planned to spend most of my time in Alaska, intending to make short work of the rest of the continental United States and Canada on the way, but curiously, I found myself dawdling in Alberta.

Alberta surprised me, enthralled me, ambushed me out of nowhere.

Medicine Hat! Head-Smashed-In Buffalo Jump! Calgary! And then there was Edmonton. Something specifically about Edmonton and its surroundings coaxed me to tarry in Alberta way longer than anywhere else, including Alaska.

Edmonton held me fast and wouldn't release me. Returning to my car from the Edmonton Zoo, I saw a man eying my license plate. "Washington, DC! Yours?"

"Yes, mine. On my way to Alaska."

"We-e-e-ll, maybe you'll make it and maybe you won't," the man answered. "I was on my way to Alaska, too. From Minneapolis. Made a stop here, and never left. That was THIRTY YEARS AGO!"

The man howled with laughter, pounded me on the back, and, still howling, made his way down the street, turned the corner and disappeared. That howl echoes in my dreams.

One noteworthy, lovely thing that happened in that town was a delightful lunch I had at a deli. The meal was wondrous and redemptive, and the hostess, a charming and enchanting young woman, made such an impression on me that, all things considered, as I left

Alberta and continued to Alaska, I said out loud, "My future is here."

Five years later, to the day, I was back in Alberta, on a farm outside of Edmonton, marrying a girl who grew up on that farm.

Some years later, in the midst of my reminiscing about Alberta and Edmonton, my wife interrupted me and asked me about the deli I'd been to. I remembered the name, and she nodded and said, "Yes, I was hostessing there that summer —so *that was probably me.*"

So travel, for me, has been more than just going from one place to another, more than sightseeing, and more than souvenirs and postcards. It is something profound, mystical, divine and demanding -- that cosmic tug, that unopened gift that refuses to spill all its secrets right away.

Travel is the oration that doesn't reach its climax until it's good and ready – even if it takes years to make its point.

Travel is destiny.

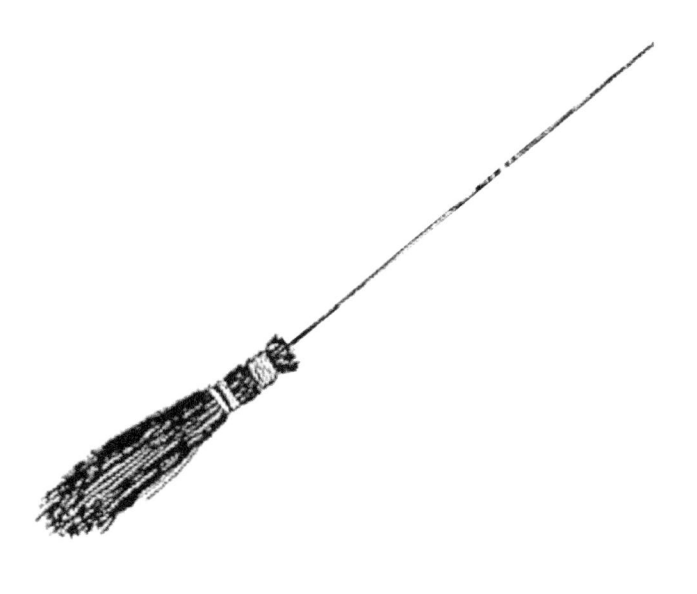

"THE NUMBER
ONE
CAUSE OF AGING
IS
STIFLED YAWNS."

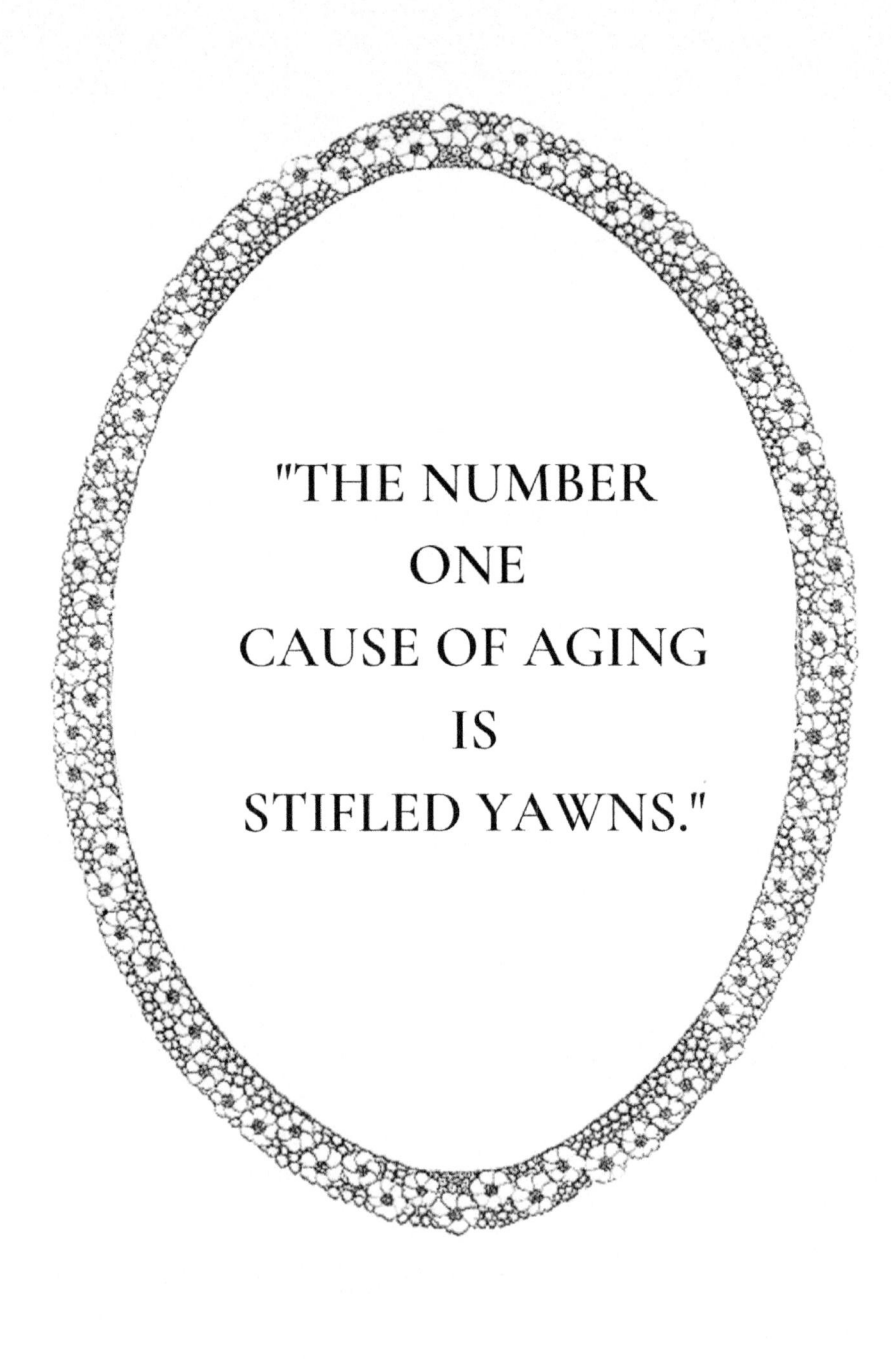

Look Young!
Be Happy!
Make Money!

Hey! My birthday's coming up! I'm getting older! And so are you! So, we're really in the same boat, you and me! But no worries! Here are three handy-dandy sure-fire tips to look younger and feel happier. And, lucky you, they ALL have to do with OTHER PEOPLE!

Tip #1: Don't be supercilious! Did you know that when you curl up your face in a suspicious, scornful or imperious look, you use 46,843 facial muscles?? Fact! That's 46,843 muscles tensing, flexing and messing up your youthful visage!

Yikes! Smiling, on the other hand, uses only TWO facial muscles!!! So smile whenever you meet, talk to or talk about someone, regardless of race, color, creed, nationality, politics, gender, or nutritional preference. Way better for face and figure!

Tip #2: Be interested! When you talk to someone, be genuinely interested. And if you aren't, don't pretend that you are. Do NOT *pretend* interest if you're not interested. Science proves this. *The Number One cause of premature aging is stifled yawns.*

Astounding but true! Stifled yawns create unsightly wrinkles and stretch marks around the mouth. Much better to simply tell the person, "I'm afraid, dear fellow, that I'm completely bored by you and your genuine Northumbrian spoke-shaver's coracle. Now, why do you suppose that is?" Do that, and watch the conversation become *really* interesting *really* fast.

Tip #3: Who's the most aggravating person in your life right now? Yes! That one! Oooh, if he/she/they/it would just. . . Don't *you go there!* Reject all inducements, provocations or invitations to harbor ill will!

And that includes invitations to be aggravated, irked, annoyed or vexed. And, you know this: some people send you *engraved* invitations, that's how much they want you to join their little grump clique. Just resist the temptation to snarlingly accept that invitation (a sure wrinkle-producer) and smile and say no thank you instead. You'll look and feel serene, and people will wonder what you're up to.

As mentioned earlier, these handy little tips all involve OTHER PEOPLE. This is cool because you will look younger and feel happier (OK, you may or may not make money—I lied), but by injecting that much more kindness and love into the world, you'll be making the rest of us feel good, too.

Give it a go, and don't say I didn't warn you.

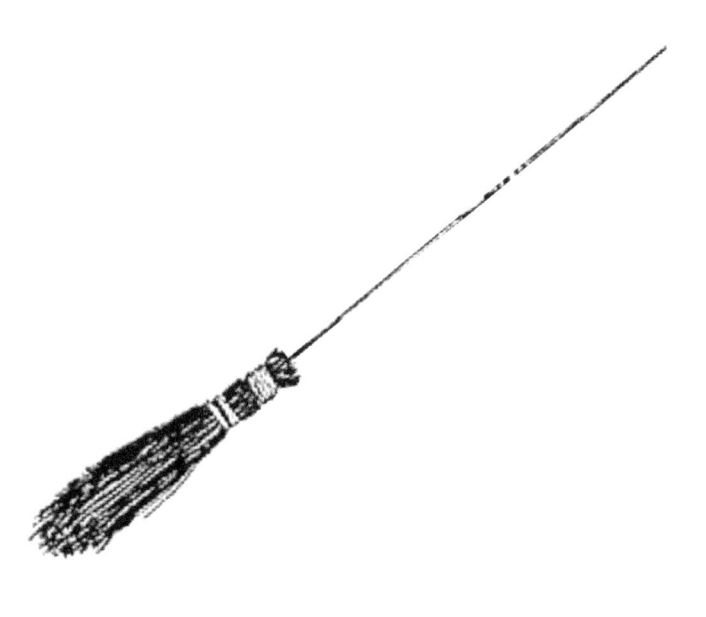

"YOU ARE IMMORTAL. YOU CANNOT DIE. OF ALL CREATIONS ON HEAVEN & EARTH, YOU ARE THE BEST, & MOST PRECIOUS."

Our Secret Angel

There's a Jewish legend about what happens to us before we are born.

An Angel appears and introduces us to all the high and low places in the world, all the great works of Nature, and all the important and trivial affairs of men.

The Angel then takes us on a preview of the life we are about to live. We are shown where we will reside, what work we will accomplish, what struggles, triumphs, loves and losses we will endure, what endeavors we will undertake and what destinies will befall us.

To be sure, there are many unpleasant and unhappy stops on our journey. We may lose heart and wish to turn back. At these difficult points, it is up to the

Angel to keep us moving until our whole life story is revealed.

At the journey's end, the Angel restores us to the womb but not before whispering the great Secret: *You are immortal. You cannot die. Of all creations on Heaven and Earth, you are the best and most precious.*

And with that, the Angel lays a loving finger on the baby's lips—as you or I would give a gentle "Shhh…" to a small child—and departs.

That is why we are all born with that slight indentation above our lips and beneath our nose. That's where the Angel laid its finger upon us, sealing the Secret within us.

That is also why a newborn baby cries, has tantrums and fusses: he has forgotten the Secret and doesn't know who he really is. He has forgotten that to find the Secret, he need only look within himself—right where the Angel sealed it.

This legend comforts me. I once suffered an immense and soul-numbing loss. With loss comes sorrow and tears—that appears to be the way things work. But reminding myself that the tears signify that I've simply forgotten for the moment who I really am, brings consolation and a measure of redemption.

After all, remembering who one really is brings as well the realization of who we all are.

We are not what they tell us in the commercials and bad jokes and the small print at the bottom of the contract. We are not tiny, frightened, confused ciphers that shatter at the smallest zephyr of adversity or change. We are not, in short, *things*.

We are beings. Beings with neither beginning nor end.

When we enter this life, everyone rejoices while we are the only ones crying.

When we let go of this life, everyone weeps while we are the only ones at peace.

Why? I like to think it's because, while at the first breath, we have forgotten who we are and must search a lifetime to remember, at the last breath, we are restored to that awareness and can depart.

Religion reminds us of who we really are—and that we can be so much more than we think we are.

Faith is the secret Angel that keeps us going, through all the struggles and heartache, to the final revelation of the truth.

The truth we knew all along.

"WHILE
IT LASTS.
GOLDEN FLORIDA
SUNSET JUICE
FIVE DOLLARS
A
BOTTLE."

Sunset Juice

Once upon a time, there was a Once-upon-a-time. He wore a white suit with a pink ribbon around the neck, pink bunny-rabbit slippers with open toes, and often walked around with his finger raised as though he had something to say.

He would then draw himself up to his full height, cough importantly, and say, "Once upon a time." After which, he would sit down and look mysterious.

People were impressed by this at first, and for a while, the Once-upon-a-time was in demand at all the best parties, get-togethers and teas.

There was Mayor Mitchell, who had parties in his office; and there was Inspector Twitchell, the Chief of Police, who had get-togethers in his living room; and there was Ms. Chitchell, the principal of the local elementary school, who had teas on her patio.

At each party the same thing would happen:

The person throwing the party would very grandly introduce the Once-upon-a-time, the Once-upon-a-time would then stand up, cough importantly, and say, "Once upon a time," look mysterious, then sit down and nod at the applause.

The Once-upon-a-time had a different speech for every occasion.

For sad occasions he would look dignified and serious and say "Once upon a time" in a slow, mournful voice as if to say that was the only hope left for the world.

For happy occasions he would chuckle, "Once upon a time," the way you or I would tell a funny story, then laugh at his cleverness.

By and by, though, most of the people who were first impressed by the Once-upon-a-time grew tired of his four-word speeches and decided that he was pretty boring after all. He got invited to fewer and fewer teas and get-togethers until at last, the only friend he had left was a small boy named Tommy, who lived on Geranium Street, across from Mr. Teena's grocery store.

Tommy liked the Once-upon-a-time because his speeches always made him fall asleep. Tommy liked sleeping better than most things because of the special world he was building in his dreams. It had the usual stuff you'd expect dream worlds to have: lions, castles, cops and robbers and fighter pilots.

But Tommy's world had some extra things in it as well. Practical things. Things like sheets and pillowcases, a change of socks, a refrigerator with cold milk and three kinds of juice inside, and an extra blanket in case it got chilly.

The Once-upon-a-time, for his part, liked Tommy for two reasons.

The first reason was that no one else in town would listen to his speeches.

The second reason was that because of Tommy, the Once-upon-time found that he had a very special and magical power: the power to make people fall asleep.

Every day the Once-upon-a-time practiced his new ability.

He practiced making people fall asleep at a distance. First, from five feet away. Then from ten feet away. Then from twenty feet. Then from a whole city block.

The Once-upon-a-time found that as he practiced, he could make people fall asleep before he got to the word "time" in "Once-upon-a-time;" then before getting to the word "a," and sometimes even on "upon."

Tommy, of course, remained the Once-upon-a-time's best audience. Just seeing the Once-upon-a-time open his mouth made Tommy fall asleep.

By and by, Tommy's mother grew worried.

She cornered the Once-upon-a-time one day and said, "Now see here. Because of you my boy is sleeping entirely too much. He's missing out on school, and I can't make his bed because he's always sleeping on it. I think you ought to stop seeing him. I think you ought to leave town and never come back. Now what do you think of that?"

The Once-upon-a-time sighed sadly and said, "Once upon a time," at which Tommy's mother fell instantly asleep.

The Once-upon-a-time was at first surprised, then delighted at this. He clapped his hands and laughed, "Once upon a time!" and then caught himself just as *he* started to fall asleep.

In the following weeks, the Once-upon-a-time and Tommy visited each other more often. And because he saw the Once-upon-time more often, Tommy got more sleep.

He slept during the nights and he slept in the afternoons.

He slept between meals and he slept during meals.

He slept on school days and he slept on national holidays.

And as he slept, he worked on his dream world.

He added more sheets and pillowcases to it, more blankets and pairs of socks, and more refrigerators filled with cold milk and three kinds of juice.

Things went along pretty well for a while, and it may have continued this way if the first remarkable thing hadn't happened.

It's hard to say how it happened or what made it happen, but one morning at about 3:30, Tommy's dream world sprung a leak.

It may have been that it just got too crowded. It may have been that Tommy had crammed in one sheet too many or one refrigerator too many.

Whatever it was, something in the clutter shoved up against the sunset in Tommy's dream world and punctured a hole in it.

(It was a big, beautiful sunset, rich and thick, like a strawberry cheesecake, if you can imagine a strawberry cheesecake colored gold and orange and red, with just a hint of purple. And though it was just a dream world sunset, it was a sunset, just the same.)

The leak wasn't noticeable at first, but by and by, little drops of sunset dripped out of Tommy's dream world and splattered on the floor beside his bed.

As the hole in the sunset grew, the drip-drip of bits of sunset became a dribble, then a drizzle, then a flow, then a gush, then a roaring torrent of sunset juice.

It streamed out of Tommy's bedroom window and into the street below in brightly-colored rivers of gold and orange and red, with just a hint of purple.

Luckily, Tommy was awake by now and knew what was going on.

He swiftly tip-toed down the steps, careful not to slosh too much sunset on the carpet, opened the door, headed down the street to the Once-upon-time's house, and knocked.

The Once-upon-a-time opened the door, looked at Tommy, looked at the sunset juice roaring out behind him, grabbed his young friend, and took him to the highest spot in town -- a statue at the other end of Geranium Street of a famous general on a horse.

With a great deal of trouble, the Once-upon-a-time pushed Tommy up on top of the horse, with the sunset juice splooshing and sploshing behind him.

By now, the sunset juice had reached the flood stage. Tommy could see it from his seat on the horse as it roared down the length of Geranium Street.

"Wake up everybody and warn them!" Tommy cried.

The Once-upon-a-time jumped off the statue and splashed down Geranium Street, knocking on doors and shouting, "Once upon a time! Once upon a time!" as loud as he could.

Naturally, on hearing the Once-upon-time, anyone who would have been awake at this hour fell immediately asleep; and anyone who was already asleep became even more so.

The situation was rather dire by now, and it may very well have gotten worse if not for the second remarkable thing.

It's hard to say how it happened or what made it happen, but that morning, at around 5:00, the leak in Tommy's dream world sunset closed up.

It may have been because it was a dream world sunset.

It may have been because everyone has a dream world, and interesting things can happen in dream worlds.

It may have been because that night Mayor Mitchell dreamed that he passed a law against leaking sunsets.

It may have been because that night Inspector Twitchell dreamed that he arrested a sunset for leaking and littering the street.

And it may have been because that night Ms. Chitchell dreamed that she made a sunset stay after school and write, "I will not leak out of turn," one hundred times on the blackboard.

Whatever it was, something stopped the flood of sunset juice by the time the town awoke that morning.

And what was left of the sunset juice was gathered up and bottled by Mr. Teena, who put a big sign out in front of his grocery store:

"WHILE IT LASTS. GOLDEN FLORIDA SUNSET JUICE FIVE DOLLARS A BOTTLE."

Mr. Teena was no fool.

Meanwhile, for some reason that no one could quite figure out, the people in the town found themselves liking the Once-upon-a-time again.

Slumber parties now became the thing to do.

There was Mayor Mitchell, who had slumber parties in his office; and there was Inspector Twitchell, who had slumber get-togethers in his living room, and there was Ms. Chitchell, who had slumber teas on her patio.

Naturally, both Tommy and the Once-upon-time were always invited.

And when the time came to go to sleep, the person throwing the party would very grandly introduce the Once-upon-a-time, who would then stand up, cough importantly, wink at Tommy (who would wink back) and say -

Now, *what* was it he would say?

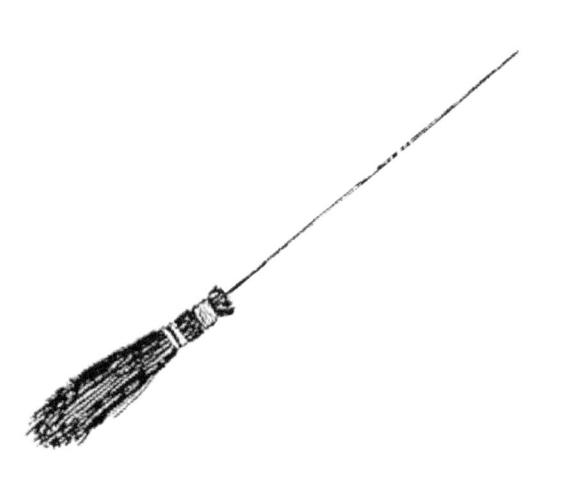

"'YOU COME,'"
SHE COMMANDED.
THE WOMAN
WAS AN ATHLETE.
SHE COULD WALK
FORTY MPH
WITHOUT
A PUFF OR HUFF."

Love Is A GPS

Our connection was a plane from Lisbon to Rome and then yet another plane from Rome to our first port of call, Catania, Sicily, Italy.

Lisbon to Rome was listed as a three-hour flight, but the unscheduled-and-unexplained-yet-vital-for-some-unfathomable-reason pre-flight wait on the ground took another hour.

While waiting, I went over some fast mental arithmetic: there's about an hour between this flight landing and the next flight taking off, so if we sit here for an hour, that means we'll have zero time to make the next plane, unless it's right next to this one, like at the same gate, a physical impossibility.

And if we miss the next plane, we'll get into Catania really late, like REALLY late, like after-midnight late, like after-all-the-cabs-go- home-and-we're-stranded-at-the-airport- helpless-and-at-the-mercy-of a cruel-and- capricious-Fate late and like we-can't-get-into the-B&B-and-so-are-forced-to-sleep-in-the- street-outside-the-gate late.

But they'll wait, I thought. They'll know people are coming in, and they'll simply hold the connecting flight for us. The other passengers will understand. It's not like THEY have to sit and wait on the ground for a whole hour like we did. Maybe just half an hour. Forty or fifty minutes. The thought comforted me.

"YOUR PLANE IS LOST," announced the airline person waiting for us at the arrival gate. She held a sign with our names and a few others on it so that all the other passengers around us, who had made THEIR flights, would know who we were and that we had a LOST

PLANE, and that somehow, some way, on some deep resonating level, it was all our fault.

"You come," she commanded and then whirled around and made her way briskly through the airport. The woman was an athlete. She could walk forty mph without a puff or huff. The younger people who had also lost their planes could barely keep up with her, but we could not keep up her pace, and she shook us within moments.

To make matters worse, I had not only lost the plane, but I had now lost my wife. We had gotten separated by the vast Rome airport crowd, and now I was alone amid a teeming swarm of tour groups, family groups, Asians, Americans and other nationalities, all eddying and flowing in all directions around me.

I had only been in the Rome airport once before – years earlier – on my way to my sister's wedding in Israel. At that time, I had been accosted by an Italian soldier with a machine gun. While accosting, he said many things to me in Italian, which, though I couldn't understand, were non-complimentary. I reflected that I really don't like the Rome airport, and though there was now no accosting Italian soldier with a machine gun, I felt no better at this moment than I did back then.

I backtracked, hoping my wife and I would somehow pick up on each other's radar. It was all I had to rely on – that crazy hope that somehow two hearts beating with the same rhythm would act like homing devices to one another.
I closed my eyes and trusted The Force (actually not – I just kept wandering in no particular direction, but confident

that we'd find each other, because—well—just because).

Could we find each other again?

We did!

I spied her! She spied me!

Excitedly, she waved me over to a counter where she, the other passengers and the airline athlete stood, the latter visibly disappointed that she had failed to elude us.

We booked a later plane and indeed arrived at the Catania airport late, but there were still lots of people and lots of taxis available, no problem – yay!

But even had there been no taxis, even had we arrived at the B&B too late, even had we needed to sleep on the street in the cold and damp—we'd still have been together. And that's all that counts when you're in love. (That, and getting the deposit back).

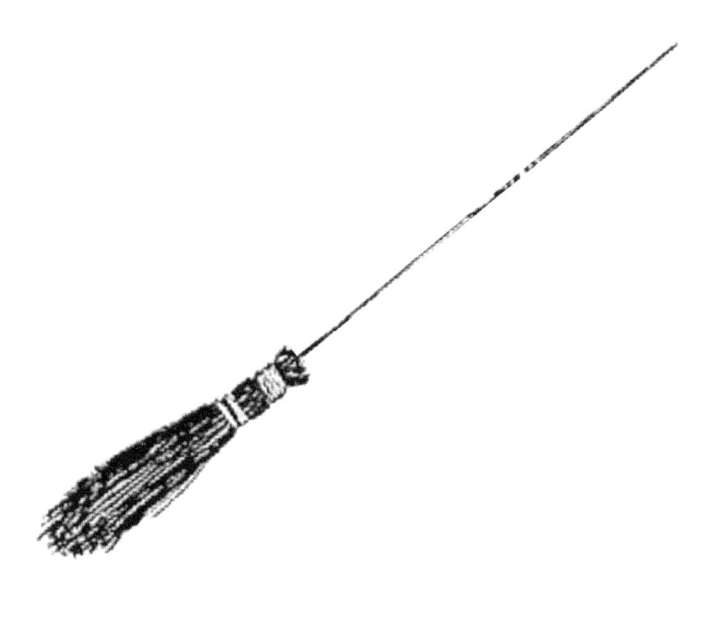

"DUE TO
A SUDDEN
REVERSE BACKSPIN
OF
THE EARTH'S
ROTATION,
LAST WEEK
WILL REAPPEAR
THIS COMING
THURSDAY."

Last Week Gets A Do-Over

Due to a sudden reverse backspin of the earth's rotation, last week will reappear this coming Thursday.

Scientists are at a loss to explain the sudden quirk in the earth's rotation. The most plausible theory to date comes from retired minor league pitcher for the Amarillo Sod Poodles, Sammy Tush.

"It's a simple matter of spit," Tush comments.

"Anyone who's ever seen a pitcher throw a spitball knows that the way the ball spins, and the way the world is spinning right now are exactly alike. Someone somewhere just spat right, that's all."

Whatever the actual reason or reasons, the reappearance of last week has been universally hailed. Now is the chance to take back that stupid thing you said to your spouse last week—or better yet, pretend it never happened because. . .well. . . it never did. . .

Were you sick last week and missed that key game? No worries! It's still on the schedule! You can still go!

You forgot to pick up a lightning rod, so your house got struck by a bolt in that thunderstorm and burned to the ground? Great news! The storm didn't happen! You've still got your house! And best of all: your insurance rates didn't go sky-high!

And those are just YOUR astonishing results of getting a second chance at last week!

Imagine the repercussions for humankind:

Millie Fitz, known as the World's Slowest Human, gets to increase her already prodigious world record of time spent rummaging for her debit card in the supermarket checkout line.

The Omaha, Nebraska City Council gets seven extra days to decide what to call people from Omaha. The hotly debated issue has been raging for months — should people from Omaha be called "Omaha-ans," "Omahaians," "Omahamians," "Omahots," or simply "People Who Come From Omaha?" Or should they just shut down the town and move someplace that ends with a consonant?

AND you get to put off that thing you put off doing last week just a bit longer. Yeah, that one.

"HOW DO I GET MY HANDS ON MY VERY OWN 7-FOOT TALL, INFLATABLE BLACK SANTA?"

Miracle In North Little Rock

Suppose your holiday shopping list this year includes a miracle. In that case, you need go no further than the little town of North Little Rock, Arkansas, population 65,000, give or take, nestled across the Arkansas River, a bridge away from its more populous sister city, Little Rock.

It was in the Lakewood area of North Little Rock where hatred was turned to love by people who didn't have to do what they did but did it anyway.

Chris Kennedy, honoring a family tradition from his childhood, wherein he would help his Dad put up Christmas decorations right after Thanksgiving, put up this year's decorations with his 4-year-old daughter, Emily. They strung up the lights and set up the inflatable Christmas tree and Black Santa on their front lawn, just as they'd done every year.

A few days later, Chris opened his mailbox and was shaken to find an anonymous letter from "Santa" containing racist threats directed at his family, his ancestry, and at the 7-foot Black Santa on his front lawn.

The letter began with the lines: "*Please remove your Christmas yard decoration,*" the letter said. "*You should not try to deceive children into believing I am a Negro. I am Caucasian, White man to you.*"

Chris reported the incident to local law enforcement and prepared his family for what they felt would be the imminent onslaught of hate, for which the venom in his mailbox was merely the harbinger.

But something different happened. Neighbors, hearing of the incident on social media, responded in solidarity. 7-foot tall inflatable Black Santas began dotting front lawns throughout

Lakewood. Christian families, non-Christian families, white families, families of color – all choosing to decorate their homes with 7-foot tall inflatable Black Santas.

And the Black Santa movement did not stop there, spreading through the town to the extent that local merchants began running in short supply of the inflatable 7-foot Black Saint Nicks. The question had changed from, "How could such a hateful thing happen in our community?" to "How do I get my hands on *my* very own 7-foot tall inflatable Black Santa?"

The tsunami of support restored Chris and his wife Iddy's faith in people. "The outpouring of love, support, and unity that we're seeing from the community has just been incredible," Chris observed. "People have been stopping by and honking. We've gotten cards, gifts and letters from different people in the neighborhood and even across the U.S."

Iddy, relieved at the turn of events, agreed. "The outpouring of support made me realize that this is the perfect place to raise our daughter. She may not understand but she definitely notices the Black Santas popping up," she continued.

"I would like to think that's a warm and fuzzy feeling. I didn't see it growing up, but the fact that it will be normalized for her gives me hope for the future."

Donations have been pouring in, including a second, even taller inflatable Black Santa that now proudly stands by the first one on the Kennedy lawn, like a big brother, a head taller than its companion. The family has redirected all donations to the Ronald McDonald House Charities of Arkansas, which, as a result, is now experiencing unexpected largess.

North Little Rock, once unfairly called Dogtown as an attempt to disparage its working-class roots, can now proudly take its place in the growing ledger of things that prove that by working together, humanity can still achieve peace on Earth and goodwill toward men.

"IF THERE IS
ANY SINGLE REASON
THAT I AM ADMITTED
TO HEAVEN,
IT WOULD BE THAT I
BROUGHT HER TO
THAT PLACE OF JOY
AT A TIME WHEN JOY
WAS SUCH
A SCARCE
COMMODITY."

The Special Place In The Northwest Corner Of My Thoughts

There is a place I return to again and again.

It's not in any physical location but tucked away in a special place in the northwest corner of my thoughts. After our oldest son died horribly and unfairly, I did as much as possible to create happy moments for my darling wife.

There was no way that any amount of joy could tip the scales of such deep, searing grief, but I tried. Five years after his death, I took us to Europe. The highlight of that trip was our journey to Monet's garden at Givenchy outside of Paris.

My wife's favorite thing in the wide world was flowers, and Monet must have had her in mind when he provided her with avalanches and eruptions of flowers--all colors, shapes, varieties and scents.

This was Eden to her—her happy place. I like to think this was the turning point from inconsolable devastation to the beginning of healing. I was lucky enough to witness the very peak moment of that day.

I still see her there, standing on the famous Japanese bridge, the centerpiece of so many of Monet's canvases, the day drunk with flowers, and she at the center—beaming at me—serene, young and fully alive. The day was cloudy and chill, but she was the sun.

I go to that time again and again and replay it. If there is any single reason that grants me entry to Heaven, it would be that I brought her to that place of joy when joy was such a scarce commodity.

We all have our special places that we can go to. Some are on the outskirts of our thoughts, and some are always right there with us. But they always appear when summoned.

For me, the place with the well-trod path in my waking and sleeping dreams is that miraculous moment in Monet's garden, right there in the northwest corner of my thoughts.

"ONCE I'VE GOT IT TOGETHER & PERFECT, I'LL SUBMIT IT TO THE UNITED NATIONS & THE DICTIONARY PEOPLE."

Peace On Earth By Tuesday!

Peace on Earth! It's so simple! How could the solution to the world's oldest riddle have eluded us for so many millennia?

Eons, epochs, periods of literature, music and fine art have all flourished and dimmed, come and gone with no one noticing that the answer had been sitting there in the corner, quietly minding its own business, hiding in plain sight until I stumbled over it, suffering only mild contusions.

 Here, then, is my plan for peace on earth. All we do is *eliminate the third person from the language!* Yes!

That's *him, her, they, them, he, she.* Gender-neutral pronouns, of course, would stay in the lexicon.

Then, once everyone's used to that, we remove the second person from the language:
YOU and YOURS.

Then, once everyone's used to *that*, we remove the possessives: MINE, YOURS, HIS, HERS, THEIRS.

That way, there's nothing left but the first person singular and plural: I, ME, WE, US and OURS.

What happens when we do that? No one can say bad things behind anyone's back anymore—because there's no
more *they* and *them* and no
more *him* and *her*.
(I still haven't decided about "*it*." Eliminating the word, *it,* would make shopping impossible, and THEN where would we be?)

We'd all have to talk TO one another. And because it's all US and WE, we couldn't blame anything on anyone. Instead of "You did that!" we'd have to say, "We did that!" And instead of, "It's MINE!" we'd have to say, "It's OURS!"

We'd all have to talk *to* one another instead of *about* each other.

An interesting wrinkle would be that we'd no longer have "I love you." It would have to be, "I love US." But when you think about it, isn't that really the way it is when you truly love someone, and you're together, and it's all beautiful and squishy?

My plan will eliminate all wars, replacing them with beach holidays.

It will also save the environment due to shorter dictionaries.

I'm still working out some bugs, but once I've got it together and perfect, I'll submit it to the United Nations and the Merriam-Webster people.

Yes, it's revolutionary, but hear me out. Remember the last time you heard someone say something unkind about you, your group, your race, or your religion? It was someone who had heard something about you or your group from someone else, right?

They hadn't heard it or seen it from YOU! Of course not!

Everything bad you've heard is precisely that: *everything bad you've heard*. The odds of hypocrisy, bigotry, distrust, suspicion, coldness and antipathy *decrease* hugely when we simply *talk* to one another.

An African American man recently put this to the test when he joined a white supremacist group. After the initial cold shoulder (and worse), he broke the ice simply by chatting, making friends, and being the regular good guy he naturally was.

Result: lots of new friends and lots of ex-white supremacists.

Really. Spread it around. If we just talked *to* each other, we would have peace on earth by the weekend—Tuesday at the latest.

With or without the pronouns.

You heard it here first.

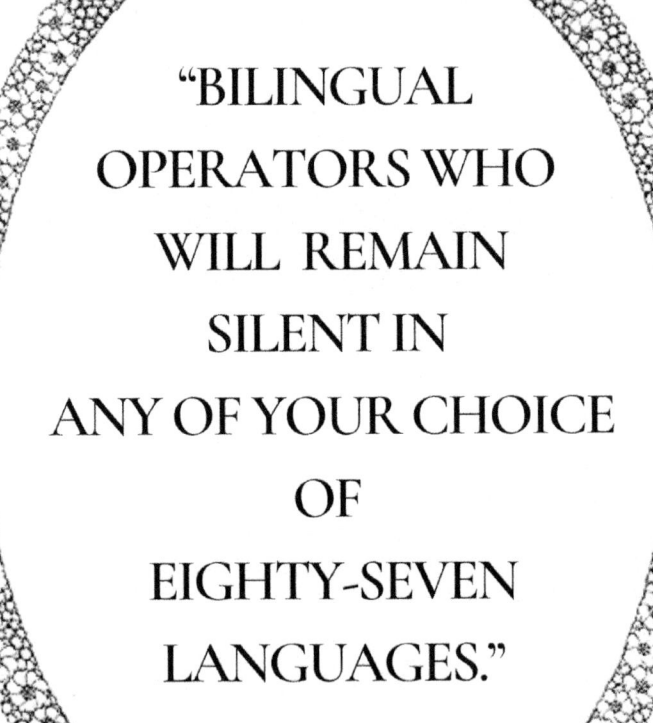

"BILINGUAL OPERATORS WHO WILL REMAIN SILENT IN ANY OF YOUR CHOICE OF EIGHTY-SEVEN LANGUAGES."

Handy Toll-Free Numbers

For those who insist the Internet is a passing fad, and as a salute to National Sneeze On People Who Eat Sushi Month, here we go with our List of Handy Toll-Free Numbers.

NERD NEWS (1-800-OHHH GEEEE) – The hotline for nerd networking. Find out the latest Latin Scrabble team scores and standings from around the world, exciting new ways to hold your glasses together, and updated lists of foods that stick to your teeth.

OUR OPERATORS ARE STANDING BY (1-800-PLEASE HOLD) -- A service for people who need operators to stand by. Simply dial the above number, wait for the tone, and press "pound." An operator will come on the line and, for a fee of $37.00 per minute, will cheerfully stand by for up to an hour and a half. Operators will say absolutely nothing while standing by. For an added fee, someone sounding like Robert de Niro will come on every fifteen minutes and say, Your call is very important to us," and then snicker. Obnoxious elevator music (seventy-three different arrangements of "Born Free," beginning with Mantovani and ending with Ice Cube) is optional, as well as bilingual operators who will remain silent in any of your choice of eighty-seven languages.

MISSING TUPPERWARE LIDS (1-800-TUPPER WHERE??) – Lost your Tupperware lid? Perhaps it was spotted by an alert citizen who turned it into Tupper Where? – a non-profit organization that reunites distressed Tupperware owners with their lost lids; or can provide you with a replacement lid that doesn't fit.

SUPPORT GROUP FOR PEOPLE WHO DIAL WRONG NUMBERS -- (1-800-999-6543, or 6548, or something close to that, depending on the handwriting) Staffed by volunteers who also have your problem, will sympathetically listen to your experiences and who will happily call you back to keep in touch with how you're doing now, but will probably dial wrong and never talk to you again anyway.

As regards these numbers and the services rendered, we make no claims, take no responsibility, want nothing to do with anything, don't know what you're talking about, don't even speak English, and would like you to go away right now before we call Bruno.

"LARRY,
THERE'S A LOT
OF LOVE
OUT THERE.
YOU'RE NOT GETTING
ANY OF IT.
DON'T YOU
WANT SOME?"

The Rabbi And The Bigot

There's a right way to do things and a wrong way to do things.

The right way to turn on a light switch is to flick it to the "On" position. The wrong way is anything else:

- Yelling at the light switch.
- Blaming the light switch for being off.
- Shooting the light switch with an assault rifle.
- Reasoning with the light switch.
- Posting guards and checkpoints around the light switch.
- Throwing millions of taxpayer dollars for a government study on why the light switch won't turn on.
- Organizing torch-lit parades to destroy all light switches

And so forth and so on and on.

In short, the right way to turn on a light switch is to simply flick it to the "On" position. Everything else is wrong.

The same applies to life.

How do we know if we're doing something the right way?

Simple. It works. OK, so what works? Well, love generally works. Trust works at least 80% of the time (which means that distrust works only 20% of the time). Discussion and education usually work—like flicking the light switch.

Doing things right makes things simple. Doing things wrong not only complexifies things but generally makes them worse.

One Sunday morning in 1991, Rabbi Michael Weisser of the South Street Temple in Lincoln, Nebraska, answered his phone to hear a voice: "Hey, Jew Boy, we'll make you sorry you moved here."

A few days later, the Rabbi found a package on his front walk containing antisemitic, pro-Nazi pamphlets and a card: "The KKK is watching you, scum."

The police tracked the message and pamphlets to Larry Trapp, the state Grand Dragon of the Ku Klux Klan, who kept a stock of loaded artillery and pro-Hitler propaganda in his apartment. They advised the Rabbi to move his family out of town.

Rabbi Weissler elected not to. Instead, he looked up Trapp's number, phoned him, waited through the venomous, hate-filled outgoing message, and then left one of his own: "Larry, there's a lot of love out there. You're not getting any of it. Don't you want some?"

Once a week, Rabbi Weissler would leave a message of love and encouragement on Trapp's voicemail. When he learned Trapp was nearly blind and unable to walk due to diabetes, he left this message: "Larry, why do you love the Nazis so much? They'd have killed you first because you're disabled."

After several weeks of leaving messages, Rabbi Weissler dialed Trapp, and instead of the usual vitriol, heard instead a click and a hoarse voice:

"What do you want!"

The Rabbi answered, "I thought you might need a ride to the grocery store."

After a long pause, the voice mumbled, "Quit bothering me."

A few nights later, Rabbi Weisser's phone rang. He could tell from the Caller ID it was Mr. Trapp.

"Hi, Larry, how are you?"

After a moment, Trapp said timidly, "I want to get out of what I'm doing, and I don't know how."

The Rabbi and his wife drove out to Trapp's apartment, moved him into their house, introduced him to their friends, cared for him, ran errands for him, and let him do some office work at the temple.

He had never wanted to hate people. His father, a towering bully, had taught him by example and beatings. He eventually renounced the Klan, apologized to the congregation and converted to Judaism.

When he died from his disabilities, scores of his new friends attended his Jewish funeral.

Hate is the wrong way to do things. Why? It doesn't work. Nor do Hate's cousins: Doubt, Suspicion and Distrust. People do have a vast potential to hate, which can be tapped. We've seen that. People also have a vast potential to love, which can also be tapped. We've seen that, too.

Rabbi Weissler used love to convert a hater into a decent human being (right). He could have run away and left the hater to hate (wrong). Was he scared? Sure.

The police thought he was crazy. His friends thought he was crazy. He himself thought he was crazy. But—as we already know—sometimes it takes courage to do what's right when everyone and everything, including your gut, tells you not to.

Sometimes simply flicking that light switch may seem like the hardest task in the universe.

But if you look over the great people in your life, you'll find that what sets them apart from everyone else is that they went ahead and, despite everything, flicked that light switch. And by doing so, banished just that much darkness from the world.

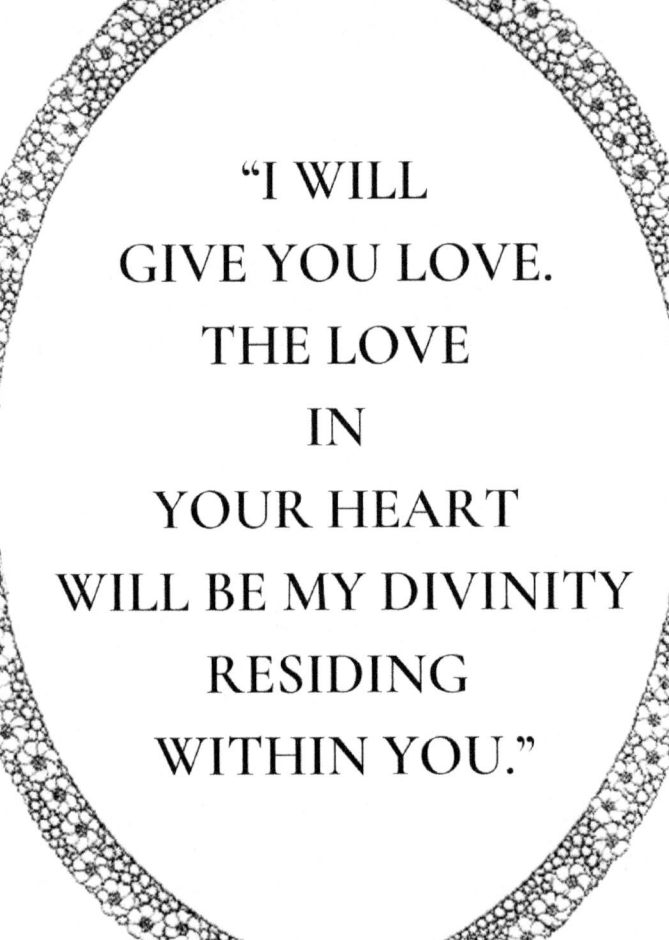

"I WILL
GIVE YOU LOVE.
THE LOVE
IN
YOUR HEART
WILL BE MY DIVINITY
RESIDING
WITHIN YOU."

The Twilight Of The Seventh Day

It came to pass, in the twilight of the Sixth Day, after God created the heavens and the Earth and all living creatures, that He realized He still had some unfinished business, and so while there was still daylight, He set about planning the miracles that were to come about in the world.

He set in motion a natural framework for the waters of the Red Sea to part precisely in time for Moses and the Children of Israel to pass through; for the sun to stand still and prolong the day for the armies of Joshua to vanquish the Canaanites in the Promised Land; for the flames of Nebuchadnezzar's fiery furnace to spare the lives of the faithful and allow them to pass unscathed.

In doing these things, he sat in council with Adam.

"Lord," said Adam, "Will You not grant us a gift — a miracle that happens not just once, but throughout eternity, as a daily reminder of Your grace and of Your presence in each person's heart?"

And God said, "I will give you Love. The love in your heart will be My divinity residing within you."

Adam answered, "May we not also have Hate, that we may appreciate Love all the more?"

And God said, "It is not for me to create hatred among men. That is a burden and a task only you can undertake."

And so it came to pass on the twilight of the Sixth Day that God created Love, while Man created Hate.

And on the Seventh Day, God rested.

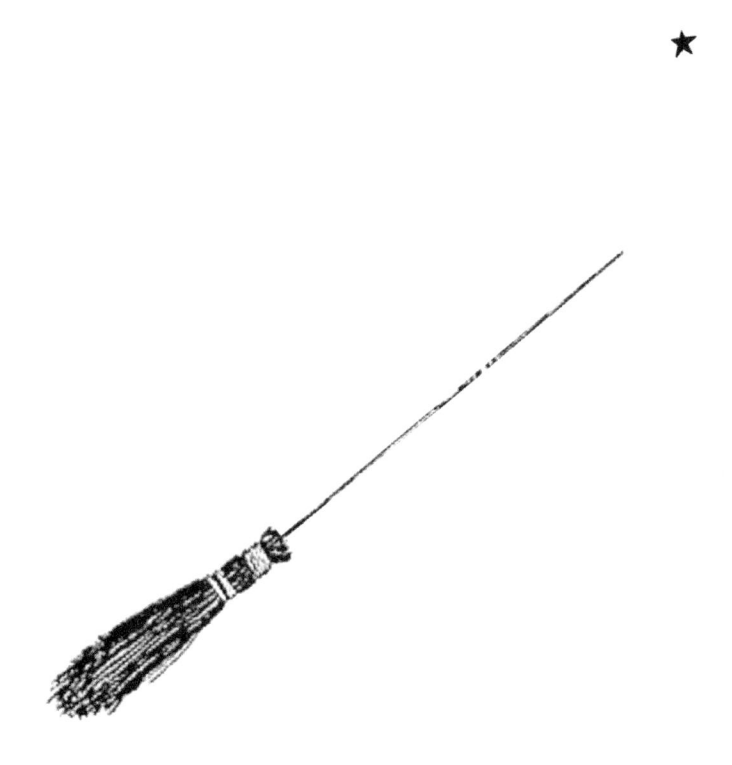

"WHEN
THE BELL TOLLED
AT
THE END OF THE FINAL
CHURCH SERVICE
EARLY THAT SUNDAY
EVENING, THE
CONGREGATION LEFT
THE SANCTUARY...
& FOUND—NOTHING.
THE HATERS
HAD LEFT."

The Benevolent Desire Of The Soul

Billings, Montana earned the nickname "Magic City," due to its explosive growth since its founding as a railroad town in 1881.

Magic City is the largest town in Montana. Though no rival in size to New York or LA, nor even Raleigh, North Carolina, Billings boasts some of the most beautiful tourist attractions in the US – from Pompey's Pillar to Pictograph Caves to Chief Plenty Coups State Park.

Billings is also home to a diverse and beautiful population, and it is they, the people of Magic City, who stood center stage that winter of 1995, the stars of a holiday miracle that has resonated through the years.

In 1995 Billings was home to 84,000 souls who lived, worked and played in their idyllic town largely outside the glare of the world's spotlight. However, early that year, there was no clue that the community was a key component in the Neo-Nazi group, Aryan Nation's plans to cleanse the Northwest five-state area of all Jews, people of color and "deviants."

Aryan Nation, in alliance with the Ku Klux Klan and other hate groups, converged on Billings in the spring of 1995. First step: Fear. Thousands of flyers distributed around town screamed, "Nuke Israel," "Jews Out!" and other such slogans. Swastikas popped up on walls, park benches and other public places. A gay man was severely beaten, Native American children were harassed on their way to school and several African Americans received death threats.

Sarah Anthony, the local human rights coalition chair, called a town meeting. Resolutions and petitions decrying hate and bigotry were swiftly drafted and passed.

Police Chief Wayne Inman urged that citizens witnessing such instances of hate and defacement should report them. County Sheriff Chuck Maxwell warned, "Don't be silent… silence is acceptance."

But the attacks only intensified. The leader of the Aryan Nation had expressed the group's strategy succinctly: "By whatever means we will purify this area. If we have to kill, we will do so." They weren't leaving Billings until their "program" was complete.

By the fall of that year, tombstones at a Jewish cemetery were overturned. Dawn Fast-Horse, a Native-American woman, woke one morning to find her house covered in swastikas and obscenities. Uri Barnea, the conductor of the Billings Symphony and the son of Holocaust survivors, sat down to dinner and heard the crash of a bottle thrown at his front door.

Klan members invaded an African-American church service, standing at the back of the room, arms folded threateningly, before leaving mid-service. When the service ended, the congregation found the outside of their church defaced with racist graffiti.

Then in early December, the miracle began. Five-year-old Isaac Schnitzer put a menorah up in his bedroom window to celebrate the Jewish festival of Chanukah. That day, a cinder block crashed through Isaac's window and landed on his bed. Thankfully, he was at school at the time. But when Isaac's

Mom, Tammy, herself a converted Jew, came home to find her son sobbing on his bed among shards of glass and the shattered menorah, she was moved to action.

She alerted the local paper, the Billings Gazette, and insisted they feature the hate crime on the front page. The Gazette's editor obliged but felt he could do more. He remembered a story he'd heard as a child about the Nazi occupation of Denmark—about how, in solidarity with the oppressed Jewish population of his country, the Danish king, Christian X, donned the yellow Star of David and urged his countrymen to do likewise.

Inspired, the editor placed a full-page image of a Chanukah menorah in the next morning's edition of the Gazette and urged the families of Billings to cut and tape the printed menorahs to their windows.

Within hours, thousands of Jewish, Gentile and Native American homes featured a menorah proudly displayed.

That night, six more homes with menorahs and a Methodist church donning the same were vandalized. But more menorahs appeared. Local businesses, stores and churches printed and distributed them. Menorahs were everywhere: in houses, trailer parks, storefronts, and places of worship of all denominations.

That Sunday morning saw a boosted African-American church attendance by the added presence of Jews, Native Americans, and others of all faiths. Moreover, teams of volunteers painted out every vestige of hate from defaced homes and public places.

And when the bell tolled at the end of the final church service early that Sunday evening, the congregation left the sanctuary into the twilight and found—nothing. The haters had left. Aryan Nation, the KKK and their brother hate groups--all gone. Overwhelmed by the town's unity and love, they'd packed up their bigotry and slinked back under their respective rocks.

Meanwhile, what happened in the Magic City did not go unnoticed. A documentary, *Not In Our Town*, chronicled the Chanukah miracle of Billings, Montana. Inspired by the Billings miracle, a Not In Our Town Movement sprang into being throughout the land that, through partnerships with schools, communities and law enforcement, helps prevent bullying and intolerance, stops hate crimes and violence, and promotes safety and harmony for everyone.

The people who participated in the miracle of Billings were somewhat surprised at all the attention their actions spawned.

The painter whose company repainted Dawn Fast-Horse's house observed, "These are our neighbors. If a brick goes through your neighbor's window, you're there, right? What's the big deal?"

And as one volunteer commented, "There's an Iroquois word, which roughly means, 'The benevolent desire of the soul.' The idea is that all of us have that benevolent desire within us. You simply have to let that benevolent desire out."

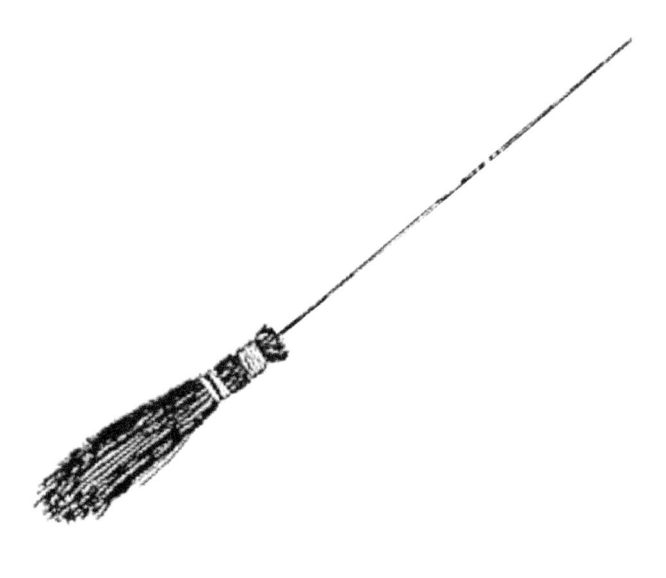

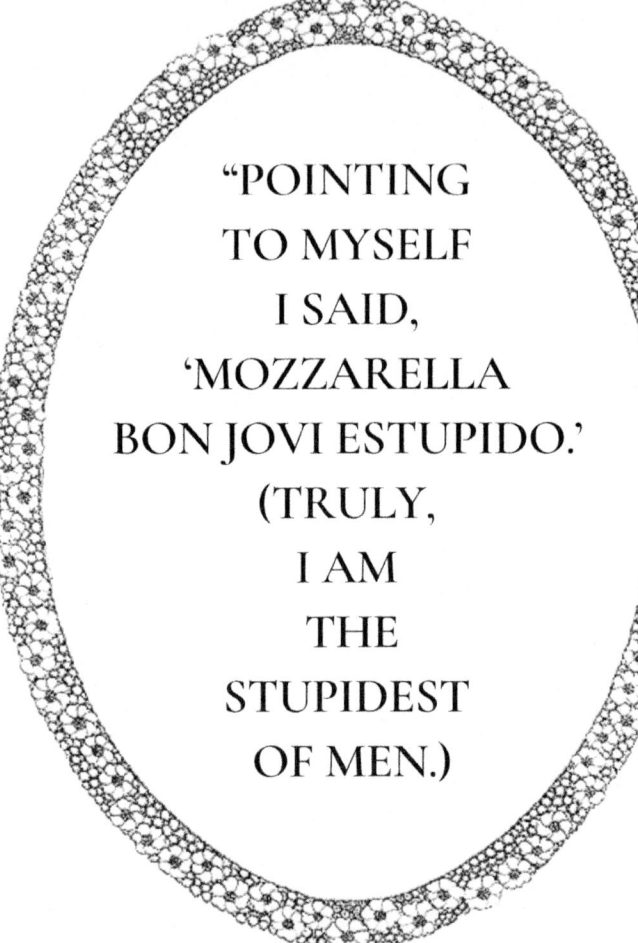

"POINTING TO MYSELF I SAID, 'MOZZARELLA BON JOVI ESTUPIDO.' (TRULY, I AM THE STUPIDEST OF MEN.)

"You Are On The Fastest Route—*BWAHH-HA-HAAA!!!*"

A trio of sea-side Southern Sicilian cities (sorry, the alliteration is just too tempting)—Noto Modica and Ragusa—form a threesome of history, aesthetics, and visual splendor that moved no less a body than the United Nations to designate the whole region an International Really Cool Area (IRCA)

It is possible that for that reason, our GPS, heretofore faithful and true while in the US, took a spin to the Dark Side. Possibly it was jealousy, misplaced patriotism or just some sick thing it had against the metric system that led it to almost, but not quite, destroy itself and us that fateful day as we sallied forth—hopeful, young and unblemished by doubt—on what we thought would be a jolly ride through the Sicilian IRCA. As we drove along rolling roads, bounded on either side by fields fertile with olive trees, carob, orange, lemon and grape and dotted by picturesque stone ruins, our friendly GPS reassured us, "You are on the fastest route. You should reach your destination by 11:43 AM."

Those were the last sane words it would utter.

 I should have suspected something was up at the first roundabout. A roundabout is like a traffic circle, only worse. Europe has roundabouts the way some people have allergic reactions. They serve the vital purpose of causing accidents and ill will among strangers.

At the first roundabout, I detected an edge in the way the GPS said, "In 100 meters, enter the roundabout and take the second exit to remain on Via King

Victor Emanuel III." I dismissed it as purely my imagination, and we thrilled at the glorious vista unfolding for us as we crossed the three-mile bridge into Ragusa.

"You are still on the fastest route," the GPS said, mid-bridge, with a touch of irony, knowing that if we turned in any direction off the King Victor Emanuel III Bridge, it was a sheer drop of 1,257 feet on either side.

The next roundabout was upon us. "Take the fourth exit," the GPS said crisply.

Wait a minute. THERE IS NO FOURTH EXIT. I turned to my wife tensely. "There are only three exits, and she wants us to take the fourth one."

"So do that," she said, unconcerned.

I made some quick calculations and figured that if I simply went around the roundabout and counted 1-2-3-4, taking the fourth exit, then that would qualify as the fourth exit, even though there were only three exits. I did that, then realized that that simply put me back towards the King Victor Emanuel III Bridge while remaining on Via King Victor Emanuel III.

The GPS maintained a stony silence, reminiscent of my 6th Grade English teacher, Miss Vernor when I misconjugated the present pluperfect of the verb "to have." At length, it spoke again, its voice distinctly hostile. "Redirecting."

Matters only got worse. The GPS had something in mind, something dark and sinister. This was not the GPS we had grown to know and love. This GPS had us at its mercy, knew it and was going to use it.

Round and round the roundabouts we went. Round in circles and U-Turns and redirections until we lost all sense of direction amidst the fantastic scenery, old cathedrals and picturesque people. Ours was a journey of doom (but really nice).

I mutinied. "I don't care what this stupid GPS says, I am going to simply Trust the Force and follow the signs back home. I want to go home!"

And with that, the GPS, sensing my revolt, changed its tone. Reassuringly it said, "You are on the fastest route. In 237 meters turn left to remain on Via Casa Grande Sacco-Vanzetti Tortellini."

I, the fool, obeyed.

In seconds we found ourselves going down a steep winding grade. It became narrower…narrower… "Go straight…"

I had to stop the car. A man at the bottom of the road was frantically signaling me. What did he want? What did he mean? I don't speak Italian hand signals. He approached me. He was an old, unshaven, simple man of the earth (as opposed to me, who by now felt more like a citizen of Uranus). It was obvious to the two of us that a car 6 feet wide is not going to fit through a road (a footpath now, actually) 2-1/2 feet wide.

Our car (an EXPENSIVE RENTED car with a MANUAL SHIFT) was pointing downward, its rear end jutting up at a 60-degree angle. There was absolutely nothing I could do. Any decision I made now would be disastrous, catastrophic. I began to talk to myself. "It won!" I moaned. "We have the GPS from hell! Devil spawn!"

The man was talking to me, possibly trying to help. Fortunately, by now, I had spent enough time in Italy to pick up some of the language. "Mama mia Corleone o solo mio?" I asked. He didn't understand. Possibly my American accent.

Then a brainstorm! My Google Translator App! Fluent in 974 languages, you just talk into it in your own language, and it comes out to the listener in the language of your choice. I motioned the man over, and we both studied my smartphone. I tapped it. He tapped it. I spoke into it: "Help us! I don't know what to do with this stupid car, and it's got an $800 deductible."

 I motioned him to listen to the phone. "*Hello! Can you tie a tie? I can tie a tie,*" it said in perfect English. The old man looked at me questioningly.

All the day's frustrations came crashing in on me. I exploded and took it out on my smartphone. "No, you stupid apparatus! In ITALIAN! It's supposed to be ITALIAN!!"

"*Can you tie an Italian tie?*" the app replied pleasantly. "*I can tie an Italian-*"

I shut it off in disgust. The old man pointed beyond me. "Mi amigo," he said.

I looked behind us and saw a sight that shall ever be ingrained in my memory: a tall, strapping young man in dusty blue jeans and a red shirt, grinning at the two of us. There was something about his manner, his bearing. He had an air about him. I knew he could help us. I believe it was Tennyson who said it best:

There was ease in Casey's manner as he stepped into his place;
There was pride in Casey's bearing and a smile lit Casey's face.
And when, responding to the cheers, he lightly doffed his hat,
No stranger in the crowd could doubt 'twas Casey at the -.

Oops, wrong poem…

The two men conferred briefly, the younger one responding with words to the effect of, "No problem." He held out his hand to me. I put the key in it. My wife emerged from the car.

The young man opened the car door, then jauntily, cavalierly dusted himself off from head to toe, chuckled, hopped in, and with the finesse of a sports car driver, put the car in reverse and tooled it back up the hill, skirting the edges by fractions of an inch, smiling all along.

I followed the car, pausing to exchange words with a simple old woman of the earth (I swear the Italian government must pay these simple old people of the earth to stand around and lend color to any situation) who was watching us curiously.

Pointing to myself, I said, "Mozzarella bon jovi estupido." (*Truly, I am the stupidest of men.*)

She patted my hand reassuringly: "Buono Capistrano mia culpa delecta." (*You haven't met my third husband.*)

The young man piloted the car to safety, alighted and gave us a little bow. I offered him money, told him I would be his slave. He laughed and waved it all off. Then, a few more parting words to the old man, a laugh, and away he went. Was it all a dream? Was this angel with a dirty face truly real? I managed to snap his photo before he disappeared into the distance as my proof that what happened was real and not an illusion.

Somehow the evil spell that had taken hold of our GPS had been broken (I'm sure by the young man in the red shirt who doubtless spends his downtime walking on water and raising the dead). The now back-to-normal GPS was as polite as could be. *You are on the fastest route,* it said, but this time it meant it.

"AFTER WE EXCHANGED PLEASANTRIES, SHE INTRODUCED ME TO HER FRIENDS IN PLOT 93, ESTHER & MOISHE, WHO SAID HELLO & GAVE ME A CABBAGE."

Yank Those Weeds!

"A recent inspection shows that you have EXCESSIVE WEEDS. You are in violation of the rules of the community garden," the letter from Sepulveda Garden Center, where my wife and I leased a 12X12 plot of earth from the City of Los Angeles began.

In the same nasty tone of voice, it then continued, *"Failure to clear your weeds within three weeks of this notice* [dated 2-1/2 weeks prior] *will result in FORFEITURE OF YOUR PLOT."*

As I didn't want to forfeit my plot (who would?) over "*EXCESSIVE WEEDS*," I was out there the next day to clear the beastly little things.

It had only been a couple of weeks since I'd last tended our garden (well, actually a month, um, no, really two months—well, three months, to be precise, yes, maybe three, maybe four.) I was, therefore, unprepared for the sight that assailed my eyes as I rounded the corner past Plots 89-90 and into our Plot, Number 91.

Our sweet little corner of rose and mint had transmogrified into a loathsome monstrosity, a tangled wilderness with weeds as high as an elephant's eye. Moreover, it had taken on a threatening aspect that made my blood run cold, congeal, freeze, thaw, liquify and evaporate.

"Oh my grandmother's smelling salts!" I gasped.

"You can say that again," came a voice to my right.

"Some people just don't tend their gardens, and that's what happens! It spoils it for the rest of us cause those weeds got *seeds* that go flying in and messing up MY garden."

It was my neighbor in Plot 92, an energetic older woman with a garden as neat and well-groomed as a maiden aunt. "I feel sorry for whoever-" she continued, then noticed the pathetic little garden trowel in my hand. "Oh, that's *your* garden. I'm sorry I was so nasty."

Her name was Mildred, she was 99 years old—older people always tell you their age—and she had been tending Plot 92 next to mine since like the Spanish-American War. After we exchanged pleasantries, she introduced me to her friends in Plot 93, Esther and Moishe, who said hello and gave me a cabbage.

I thanked them and said that considering what I had done to the neighborhood, I was surprised they didn't greet me with pitchforks, let alone a cabbage. Mildred smiled. "We've all got weeds," she said. "It's just a fact of life. Yank 'em out by the roots, or they all come back. And weeds got *seeds* that go flying in and messing up OTHER PEOPLE'S gardens."

As I hacked and yanked the afternoon away, upgrading my plot from a Black Hole of Death to merely a community health hazard, I reflected on Mildred's words: *We've all got weeds. . .Yank 'em by the roots. . .Weeds got seeds. . .*

She's right, I reflected. *We all have weeds.* Weeds in our minds, weeds of doubt, of reaction, of reluctance to let something new in the door. And yes, you must yank them out. Otherwise, you get a colossus of overgrown creeping thistle,

chickweed and ragwort that chokes out the beautiful, sweet flowers of your thought and creativity.
And don't just snip away the tops so you can see daylight.

Yank 'em out by the roots, Mildred said.
And that takes some doing because some of those roots can be mighty stubborn.

And weeds got *seeds*.

It all starts with your thoughts, your own secret garden within. You don't want to let excessive weeds overgrow your plot. Because that's when you get those nasty warning notices, and who wants those? So, get a firm grip, take a deep breath and YANK.

"THEN WITH A DISMISSIVE WAVE OF THE HAND, HE SAID, "BYE-BYE," IN A CURIOUSLY HIGH-PITCHED LITTLE BOY VOICE, & CALLED ON HIS NEXT VICTIM."

Bye-Bye!

We were at a train station in Italy. I got confused--a predictable enough outcome when it's 6 am, and you've been lugging luggage for blocks in the wrong direction after being dropped off by a cab at the wrong train station and not knowing how to speak Italian anyway.

We had two tickets each, first from Catania to Siracusa and then from Siracusa to Pozello. These are actual names, I swear.

Then at Pozello, a cab was to take us to our destination, the resort at Scicli in the province of Ragusa. My confusion was that our ticket had the train to Siracusa leaving at a way different time than the big board indicated. And to make things more confusing, ANOTHER train for a DIFFERENT TOWN ENTIRELY -- Presto Vivace – (OK, I might have made that one up) was leaving on the track OUR train was supposed to be on AT THE SAME TIME.

I explained all this to my wife and how I didn't want us to arrive at Presto Vivace when we should be at Siracusa. She said, "So go to the ticket guy and ask him."

I went there, waited in line, and when it was my turn, I shoved my ticket through the window and told the ticket guy, a gruff-looking disapproving fellow, "I just want to do the right thing."

The ticket guy looked at me without changing his gruff-looking disapproving expression. I explained to him that the time on my ticket and the time on the big board were different and that I didn't want to leave with the Presto Vivace people because I belonged with the Siracusa people.

I didn't know if he understood English as he still hadn't spoken. At length, he pointed at the big board. "You are look at *Arrivals*. *Arrivals* is *different* from *Departures*. *You* departure. *Not* arrival."

He then sounded out each syllable so I would really get it: "*Uh-RYE-Vul*. [pointing at the right side of the big board] *Dee-PAR-Cher*." [pointing at the left side of the big board]

And there it was, right on the **Departure** side of the big board: the right time, with the added bonus of the correct destination, too. "Oh," I said.

Then with a dismissive wave of the hand, he said, "Bye-Bye," in a curiously high-pitched little boy voice, and called on his next victim.

I went back to my wife and sat down. "Sometimes I amaze even myself, "I said.

I told her the whole story, ending with "Bye-Bye," complete with little boy voice and dismissive wave. She laughed and laughed. She laughed so hard she attracted the attention of two little Italian girls seated nearby who thought we were amusing idiots and offered us each a potato chip.

I took mine and ate it. My wife said no thank you. I said "Bye-Bye" to her again. She laughed and laughed. I said it many times, and each time she laughed and laughed. The little girls laughed, too. The little girls' mother didn't think it was funny and discreetly inched her little charges away from us.

Bye-Bye became for us, ever after, a motto, an anthem, a secret code meaning, *Uh oh: Stupidity dead ahead.*

The whole episode proved yet again the incalculable value of finding things out for sure, even at the price of abject humiliation because, hey, you're never going to see any of these people again anyway, right? *Right??*

"THE PRINCESS, SEEING THE IDEA'S ROUGH & ILL APPEARANCE, ASKED IT INSIDE & GAVE IT SHELTER & A WARM BLANKET & A BIT OF PORRIDGE..."

The Princess
And The Dark World

Once upon a time, when stars and sunsets were still in fashion, and the world had not yet lost its glow of pristine wonder, there lived a Princess. A wondrous, one-of-a-kind Princess she was: Princess of All The Things You Can Neither See Nor Touch But Only Believe In.

One morning as she gazed out her window, seeing nothing, of course, but feeling only hope, joy, faith and love, an Idea came knocking.

It was a strange Idea, one she'd never encountered before, but, as it was, after all, a stranger, she welcomed it into her world, just as you or I would welcome a stranger that came knocking.

Though muddy from wind and rain, the Idea went something like this: "If I can feel hope, then why not despair? If I can feel joy, then why not sorrow? If I can feel faith, then why not doubt? And if I can feel love, then why not hate?"

Seeing the Idea's rough and ill appearance, the Princess asked it inside and gave it shelter, a warm fire, and a bit of soup, just as you or I might give shelter and soup to a stranger on our doorstep who appeared chilly and unwell.

In the fullness of time, the Idea gained strength and vigor and decided to depart the Princess' domain to seek its fortune. Bidding farewell, the Idea asked the Princess what it could do to repay her kind attention.

The Princess answered, "You need not remember me. Just remember there is kindness at the heart of all hope, joy, faith and love."

The Idea knelt and kissed the Princess' proffered ring.

"I will remember," it said and went off into the world.

Many sunsets, storms and tides passed, and the Idea flourished and gained dominion in the world. People saw that hope could become despair, joy could become sorrow, faith could turn into doubt, and even love may sour into hate.

They not only saw these things, but some profited by them, sewing greed and falsehood into the Idea and thus multiplying by a thousand thousands the grief and dismay of the world.

And the Idea did not remember that kindness is at the heart of all hope, joy, faith and love, and so it broke its promise to the Princess, doubting, in the end, that there had even been a Princess at all, or that there were things that you can neither see nor touch but only believe in.

And the world became cold and dark as those who still believed in things that could not be seen or touched grew few and huddled together for warmth and light.

And the Princess of All The Things You Can Neither See Nor Touch But Only Believe In gazed out her window, seeing nothing, but feeling a heaviness in her heart, just as you or I might feel when our dreams have taken a wrong turn or two.

And then one morning, an Idea came knocking.

It was a strange Idea, one she'd never encountered before, but, as it was, after all, a stranger, she welcomed it into her world, just as you or I would welcome a stranger that came knocking.

The Idea, though muddy from wind and rain, went something like this:

"Understanding."

Just that.

"Understanding."

Seeing the Idea's rough and ill appearance, the Princess asked it inside and gave it shelter, a warm blanket, and a bit of porridge, just as you or I might provide shelter and a bit of porridge to a stranger on our doorstep who appeared chilly and unwell.

In the fullness of time, the Idea gained strength and vigor and decided to depart the Princess' domain to seek its fortune. Bidding farewell, the Idea asked the Princess what it could do to repay her kind attention.

The Princess had grown wiser with experience, so her answer to this Idea was different. "You, Understanding, shall henceforth be my Emissary to The World. Whenever and wherever there is despair, sorrow, doubt and hate, you will appear as the Path toward hope, joy, faith and love, even if only those who see you will take it."

Understanding knelt and kissed the Princess' proffered ring.

"I will obey," it said and went off into the world.

And Understanding kept its promise to the Princess.

And so, from that day until this one, it is so.

If you or I see or feel despair, sorrow, doubt or hate within ourselves or others, simply taking the path to understanding will lessen despair and let hope return.

Simply taking the path to understanding will ease sorrow and open the door one day to joy.
Simply taking the path to understanding will allay doubt and allow faith to spring anew.

And only by taking the path to understanding can we eliminate hate, replacing it with kindness and love so that we may all truly live happily ever after.

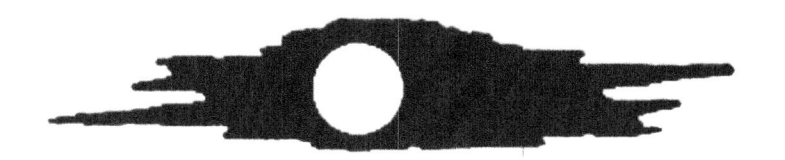

THE END

BEEEEEP!!!!, Happy Thanksgiving Every Day, The Odyssey of The Soul, Miracle In North Little Rock, Peace on Earth by Tuesday, The Rabbi and the Bigot, The Twilight of the Sixth Day, The Benevolent Desire of the Soul, Yank those Weeds! and The Princess and The Dark World were previously published in standleague.org

OUR CONTRIBUTORS

An enchanting teller of tales in her own right, Sara Baker delights in collecting the amusing & reassuring stories of others.

Martin Landon is an author, speaker & personal coach. He's written for the stage, screen, TV, online & the funny papers, & is a Practicing Optimist.

John Evans has written for theater & the big screen. His essays, fiction & poetry have appeared in several publications on the East & West Coasts.

Norm Shannon loves writing & helping in any way he can. He recently moved to Florida where he was delighted to learn they have air conditioning.

Printed in Great Britain
by Amazon